Sigmund Englander

The Abolition of the State an Historical and Critical Sketch of the Parties Advocating Direct Government, a Federal Republic, Or Individualism by Dr. S. Engländer

Sigmund Englander

The Abolition of the State an Historical and Critical Sketch of the Parties Advocating Direct Government, a Federal Republic, Or Individualism by Dr. S. Engländer

ISBN/EAN: 9783741183324

Manufactured in Europe, USA, Canada, Australia, Japa

Cover: Foto ©Andreas Hilbeck / pixelio.de

Manufactured and distributed by brebook publishing software (www.brebook.com)

Sigmund Englander

The Abolition of the State an Historical and Critical Sketch of the Parties Advocating Direct Government, a Federal Republic, Or Individualism by Dr. S. Engländer

THE

ABOLITION OF THE STATE

AN

HISTORICAL AND CRITICAL SKETCH OF THE PARTIES
ADVOCATING DIRECT GOVERNMENT,
A FEDERAL REPUBLIC, OR INDIVIDUALISM

BY

Dʀ S. ENGLÄNDER

LONDON
TRÜBNER & CO., 57 & 59 LUDGATE HILL
1873

CONTENTS.

ABOLITION OF THE STATE.

A Chapter in the History of Democracy.

———◦◦———

CHAPTER I.

THE INSURGENTS AGAINST STATE AND GOVERNMENT.

THE future historian of the democratic and revolutionary movement on the Continent will be obliged to point out that in it the mainspring was the free development of the individual. In France, Germany, and Spain the Fetish-worship of the Government has in the extreme circles of democracy entirely ceased, and we can, in fact, almost call the most advanced section of the party of Progress the party of the Ungovernables.

For some time past Continental democrats have sought to discover a system which shall reconcile the autonomic liberty of the individual with the

A

social principle; and it was held to be possible
that the activity of the individual moves freely,
not only for the furtherance of his personal
interests, but also for all collective interests,
without being hemmed in by a political fiction
or by an external power.   As soon as unrestrained individual liberty maintains itself,
and all the political and social functions are
performed without the aid of any power —whether
that power be legislative, executive, or judicial—
and are exercised by a communal and national
association, from that moment the traditional
idea of the State and Government ceases to
exist.   The State is then reduced to a simple
realisation of the will of the people by delegates,
elected for a certain time and for certain specified
objects.

All systems which aim at the abolition of the
State, aim therefore at transforming the State
into a species of joint-stock company. Although
every individual of this national association,
which thus steps in in place of the State, will
retain his unlimited liberty, yet in general affairs
he can only so far take his share in the decisions
arrived at as a unit of the public power, just as
is the case with a shareholder. Only such an
arrangement of society is considered to be
compatible with the liberty of all the members;
and thus it was that the author of one of these new

systems chose the words of Milton, "Amongst unequals no society," as the motto of his scheme. All modern systems for the abolition of the State protest against the possibility of laws being passed in a free society by a national representation. They quote Rousseau, who opined "that to give laws to mankind gods would be necessary;" and only those societies are regarded as free by these modern reformers, of whom we shall have to speak, in which all the citizens, either by adopting or rejecting the laws proposed, have directly taken part in the legislation.

The anti-Governmental and anti-State school desire to put an end to the era of imposed authority, and of a state of things in which the governing and the governed coexist, and demand that society can effect nothing without previously obtaining the assent of the majority. But as this majority would in nearly every case vary, the idea of a majority and a minority in society would cease to exist; and it therefore could not be said that the latter were tyrannised over by the former.

All modern reformers who have demanded the abolition of the State, wished thereby to point out that the State should be transformed into a species of parish. Emil de Girardin has most consistently carried out this view; when extending a proposition of Olinde Rodriguez, he simply

moved that all the electors of France should
only write one name upon a voting-paper, and
that the candidate who thus received the greatest
number of votes should be proclaimed "Maire
de France." The eleven following candidates,
in the order of their votes, should form a
"commission nationale de surveillance et pub-
licité."

The conception of the State as a parish, and,
indeed, as an agglomeration of parishes, is held
by these anti-State reformers to assist in the
emancipation of the individual from the State.
It is singular that this extreme party was far
sooner reconciled to the idea of a government
than to the idea of a national representation.
Helvetius it was who first aroused this antipathy
to legislative assemblies. He gave as his
reasons: "It is because they seek to interfere in
everything that there are so many laws. If it
were only desired to protect the good against the
bad, to assure to every one his property, &c., the
requisite laws would be but few, and could be
applied to all the inhabitants of the earth."

Moreover, all the systems which we have to
consider agree further in regarding as the basis
of society the sovereignty of the individual,
and thus, by the permanent co-operation of all
individuals in legislation and administration, to
transform society into a collective sovereignty.

St Simon was the first who already in the year 1818 understood the progress of history sufficiently to see that by degrees all government is transformed into simple administration, and that every one would then be producer and consumer, citizen and prince. Since then the simple negation of the Government has been pronounced by many writers. But it was only in a few of the systems in which the abolition of the State of the present day was represented as a possibility. The masters were nursed on the ideas of Jeremy Bentham, and he it was who introduced into the world the notion of a political and social egotism, and the enforcement of the rights of the individual. For sixty-one years, from 1771 until 1832, did he daily and uninterruptedly work out this idea in his numerous writings.

There is in social science one mysterious point —namely, that one which makes clear to us how much each individual loses by the social tie, how much the individual vigour of the individual must be stifled in order that its one-sided development should not frighten society, how many corpses society requires for its maintenance.

Hitherto there has been no reconciliation between the absolute right of the individual and society. Bentham sought to discover it in the principle of utility, and only recognised the laws,

the State, and society in so far as they were useful to each separate individual. Bentham scoffed
at one man sacrificing himself for another; he
transformed the whole existence of a man into
a constant calculation in favour of egotism, and
judged all and everything in accordance with its
degree of usefulness to mankind. Society and
civilisation had in Bentham's eye no other cause
of existence than the individual, and it was
his opinion that the education of the individual
had still to be commenced.

The apotheosis of the individual which emanated from Bentham, made its way not only into
the revolutionary philosophy of Germany, but
also of France ; and even in the time of Bentham
there were many thinkers who commenced to
shake the pillars of the State, and to criticise the
great tribute we have to render unto it. One of
these was Royer-Collard, who complained that
civilisation had attained such a height that all
affairs which were not our private affairs had
become State affairs.

The traditions of the first French Revolution
have also helped to make clearer the negation
of government. At the time of Robespierre even
the idea was mooted, that every public act should
be submitted to the ratification of the 36,000
Communal Assemblies. Robespierre, who saw
that the work of revolutionary demolition could

only emanate from the dictatorship of a single Assembly, knew no other means of replying to their idea except by the answer, that the sovereign people had no time to look after their own affairs, and left them therefore to their representatives.

In article 6 of the Declaration of the Rights of Man in 1791, it said, " All citizens have the right either personally or by their representatives to co-operate in the formation of the laws." Another article laid down the rule that "society has the right to call every one of its public agents to account for his administration." It was remembered that Sieyes had proposed the article, " Every society can only be the free work of an agreement of all its members." The Convention in June 24, 1793, issued a decree calling upon the people directly to govern itself. Only this direct government was postponed until "after the peace." The same Constitution laid it down 'that every resolution of the National Assembly should be despatched to all the parishes of the Republic with the title of "proposed law," and that it should come into force forty days after the despatch of such resolution, and then only in case that it had not been opposed in more than one-half of the departments; should, however, such be the case, the Primary Assemblies were to be summoned by the Legislative Body. Still the system of direct government was only to be introduced "after the peace," and has never been carried out.

The idea of a jury instead of a judicial power, and an administration instead of a government, was also frequently mooted during the first years of the Revolution. Countless passages from the speeches and motions of the time could be adduced as a proof. St Just said: "The rights of man were in Solon's head; he did not write them down, but he introduced them practically. Liberty must not be in a book: it must be in the people themselves, and must be practically carried out."

In 1793 Anacharsis Cloots said: "Properly speaking, there is only one power—that of the sovereign people. As soon as we shall have perfected our organisation by universal union, that same day will free us from what we call government. A Legislative Assembly, consisting of one or two deputies from each department, would be sufficient to superintend the small number of public offices, which, by the progress of civilisation, could be still further diminished."

Besides this, it was the opinion of Cloots that the Legislative Assembly should even appoint the ministers, thus transforming the government machine itself into an administration.

We have already mentioned that the ideas of

Robespierre himself on popular sovereignty were
modelled on those of J. J. Rousseau. Rousseau,
in his " Contrat Social," said : " The deputies
of the people cannot be its representatives ; they
are only its commissioners, and can decide
nothing definitely. Every law which has not
been personally ratified by the people is invalid :
it has no legal force." It is therefore natural
that even Robespierre himself held this idea.
He remarked : " The *mandataire* cannot be a
representative. It is an abuse of words, and
already in France we are commencing to discard
that error." The merit of having invented the
formula, " Direct Government of the People,"
which again cropped up after the February
revolution, belongs also to a man of the first
French Revolution, one of the clearest thinkers
of the age, Hérault de Secherelles.

Although the men of the Convention had thus
recognised the sovereignty of the individual, yet
they abolished it again for the benefit of the
mass; and even Rousseau, in his " Contrat
Social," which is merely an approach to liberty,
but returns afterwards to authority, arrives at
the same result.

Nevertheless, in the ideas of the Convention
is found the mental pabulum for the ideas of the
nineteenth century, which consists in merging the
political, governmental, military, and feudal in

the economic and intellectual system; so that
one tooth after another should be extracted from
government, and decentralisation brought to its
highest pitch. France had thus commenced to
tread the path to liberty by its representative
system.

The Parliamentary system, introduced into
France in 1814, as an imitation of the English
Parliament, had a false origin. But what could
eventuate in France from an imitation of the
English parliamentary system? How correct
was Elias Regnault when he said: "What does
the Chamber represent with us? With your
monetary franchise, it is not a democracy; with
your merchants and bankers, it is not an aristocracy: neither general nor special principles are
thus represented."

The French Chambers at no time represented
the country. The more the power of the Press
grew, the less importance had the Tribune. The
unsatisfactory nature of the prevailing representative system was more and more recognised
in France. And as wealth was the condition on
which a man could be elected a member of the
Chamber, materialism became the sole basis of
the Government.

It is superfluous to refer to the corruption and
rottenness which the February revolution over-
threw. It fell to the lot of Lamartine to find a

catchword for the situation. In 1839 already he said : "France is weary. In your system there is no need for a statesman : a curb only is wanted." At the banquet at Mâcon he spoke of the February revolution, the approach of which he announced as "the revolution of contempt." When the same man, on the flight of Louis Philippe, said in the Chamber of Deputies, " How is a new Government to be found ? By going to the lowest stratum of the people, of the country. By extracting from the national right that great mystery of universal sovereignty whence spring all order, all liberty, and all truth,"—all France was convinced of the necessity of appealing to universal suffrage and the representative system in order to arrive at the truth.

But as soon as the elections of the members of the Constituent Assembly had taken place, it was at once seen that universal suffrage, when brought into connection with the existing State machine, resembled a beautiful head on an ugly body; and that the people, as soon as it had voted, at once retired ; and authority was re-established on just as absolute a footing as under an absolute monarchy.

The Constituent Assembly had, therefore, scarcely met when protests against it came in from all sides; and almost immediately after its meeting, Huber made an attempt to dissolve it. The people felt that its representatives did not represent it.

At the time several books and pamphlets appeared in which the negation of government was advocated. One of the most interesting was a pamphlet by Bellegerarrigue, entitled, "Au fait! Au fait! Interpretation de l'Idée democratique." He investigated the cause of the overthrow of Louis Philippe, and he saw in the Revolution not only the fall of the kingdom, but also of the Government which had enslaved liberty. "With liberty of speech and of the press," he said, "we had abolished the Ministry of the Interior, which fettered us for the good of the king. With liberty of education the Ministry of Public Worship must cease, which was created to organise our education for the benefit of the king. With the freedom of exchange the Ministry of Commerce must be done away with, the object of which is to place public credit in the hands of the king. With the freedom of labour, the freedom of the soil, and the freedom of removal, we should have abolished the Ministries of Public Works, Agriculture, and War. France could come to herself, and return to the system of parishes."

Bellegarrigue thought there were two things which from the standpoint of public right should be kept in view: these were, the suppression of crimes against the person and property, and the defence of the State territory; and these interests alone would make a head to society admissible.

Rittinghausen, who had joined the school of Fourier, introduced the acuteness of German dialectics into the controversy on the principles of government. He showed that the representative system was a relic of ancient feudalism, and only justified when French society was a combination of corporations of all kinds who could give their deputies a special mandate. The general interests of the people cannot be represented by a special interest. National representation is nothing but a fiction, the delegate only represents himself. During the elections intriguing persons have always a preponderance over honest people, and the elected members change their views as soon as they have entered the Assembly.

Rittinghausen, therefore, proposed direct legislation as a solution. He wanted the people to divide themselves into sections, each composed of a thousand citizens, and each electing its own President. After each debate every citizen should vote. The President should then acquaint the Mayor of the district with the result of the vote, whose province it would be to com-

municate the total result of the entire vote to
a higher official, who in his turn would send it
on to the Prefect, and from the Prefect it would
reach the Minister. The latter could then
announce the vote of the whole country. When
the citizens should demand a new law upon any
subject, the Minister should be compelled to
summon the people to vote upon it within a
given time; and as soon as the views held by
the various sections were known, a commission
should clearly and distinctly draw up the law.

Rittinghausen refuted the statement that the
people did not possess sufficient knowledge, by
saying that only wholesome common-sense and
honesty were needed, and the existing Legislative
Assembly had produced nothing either noble or
beautiful. Direct legislation would, on the other
hand, call into play the entire intellect of the
people, of which a large portion under present
circumstances lies, as it were, fallow. It could
be seen from popular meetings that the people
conducted their debates with far more calmness
and dignity than the Legislative Assemblies,
and therefore no disturbances were to be feared.
Rittinghausen found it easy to refute the objection that the people could not afford sufficient
time for legislation, as he demonstrated that in
a single sitting the people could settle the
question brought forward for their decision.

The only thing which Rittinghausen admitted was, that direct legislation did not come up to the ideal of liberty, since the minority would be still forced to obey laws which they disapproved. " Thus much," he said, " one must acknowledge that direct legislation is only a step towards the brilliant future of the liberty of mankind."

The more the absolutist Buonapartist rule—which, despite the Republic, became possible—drove the Republicans to desperation, the more seductive did the idea of a direct government appear to many as the realisation of the ideal of that liberty, for which mankind had striven for so many centuries. Victor Considerant, who stood at the head of the poor Fourierists, and who, amid the universal tumult of the time, began to be ashamed of their *Phalanstère*, publicly apologised to the French nation for his school not having earlier hit upon this idea.

Considerant was so thoroughly convinced that this must be the solution, that he published a brochure entitled " La Solution, ou le Gouvernement direct du Peuple." Yet in order to point out that his great master Fourier was also acquainted with direct government, although he might not have held it advisable to publish it to the world, he placed the following words of Fourier as the motto at the beginning of his book :—

" *Si vous voulez soustraire le grand nombre à l'oppression du petit nombre, cherchez l'art de corporer le grand nombre et de lui donner une puissance active qui ne soit jamais deleguée.*"

Considerant complained that it was true that democracy maintained the sovereignty of the people, but that hitherto democracy had always desired that that sovereignty should always be delegated. This delegation of authority was simply an abdication by the people of their rights, and therefore, if the people would retain their sovereignty, they must themselves exercise it. Every law is based upon a principle: the people in the parishes must vote that principle; the votes would be publicly counted in every section. The results of the entire voting would be reckoned up, and the real direct vote of the people would then be the law. After that, the law embodying that principle would be formulated, and this would be done by a ministry elected by the people. The draft would have to be in exact accordance with the will of the people, otherwise the law would be at once rejected and the ministry dismissed.

Considerant said: "I will have a real sovereignty of the people, and no delegation of this sovereignty under any form or on any pretext. I will that the law shall always be the actual expression of the will of the people." He admitted that the people might elect a Central Assembly, a *Gérance*, or any other kind of organ; but always conditionally that the sanction of the people must be a *sine qua non* of its legality. With this presupposition, the political central institution would be only a committee of the General Assembly of the people. This committee would possess as little political power as the committees elected by the present Assemblies, which also prepare bills which receive their legalisation by being accepted by the Assembly. The Central Committee proposes the bills, but it would not be necessary that a vote should be taken on each single one. If within a certain given time the proposition of the committee should not be opposed by a specified number of the sections, that would be taken as a sign of agreement, just as much as a formal vote on the subject. Unimportant questions would thus be settled by silent consent. Under the system the national *Gérance* would be an office and not a power, and the people themselves would govern either by non-opposition or by assent. Considerant summed up his doctrine in the words : "No delegation, direct exercise of the sovereignty of the people by the people."

We have just seen that Considerant as well as Rittinghausen would have no delegation of authority, and that the former would submit

B

every bill to the 37,000 parishes of France, and
the latter to the sections of the people, each
composed of 1000 citizens.

The third system was that of Ledru-Rollin,
who also, in 1851, turned his attention to the
system of direct government, but proposed its
execution in a manner which was objected to
by Considerant. Ledru-Rollin proposed in
place of an Assembly of National Representatives an Assembly of Commissioners, who should
be only elected to draw up bills, upon which,
however, the vote of the people should always
be taken. It was difficult for Ledru-Rollin
to separate himself from his dictatorship ideas.
He allowed the Assembly of Commissioners
to issue decrees upon unimportant questions
which might not need the assent of the people.
And further, as the vote of the people could be
only either Yes or No, it could not be said that
by his system the people co-operated in the
framing of the laws.

All the journals took up the question; and
papers like *La Feuille du Peuple*, of which thou-
sands of copies circulated among the peasants,
accepted this doctrine, and introduced it even
into the peaceful circles of the country population.
Two representatives of the people, Savoye and
Bertholon, started a journal called *Le Vote
universel*, in which the necessity for a direct

government was developed. All the workmen's
journals advocated the abolition of the Presidency, and spoke in favour of direct government;
and the democratic party in France, which after
the February revolution dissolved into so many
fractions that there were at one and the same
time four distinct schemes for a dictatorship, was
now almost united, because the governing power
for which they had all striven would by this
means vanish altogether. The *Voix du Proscrit*,
which was the organ of most of the exiles,
announced that all political refugees were
unanimous on the subject of direct government.

A committee, composed of the editors of
the *Revue*, the *Liberté de Penser*, *l'Evene-
ment*, and other journals, was formed, who
for months discussed the basis on which the
future Republic was to be founded. The most
prominent members of the committee were
Bellonard, Benoit, Charassin, Chouippe, Erdan,
Fauvety, Gilardeau, Renouvier, Sergent, &c.
All these names are to be found in the volumi-
nous work which contains the collection of the
decrees for the organisation of the Republic for
direct government, and the commentaries thereupon, and which appeared in Paris in 1851,
under the title of "Gouvernement direct.
Organisation Communale et Centrale de la

Republique.   Projet presenté à la Nation."
The arrangement of the communes, public
instruction, the judiciary, finances, and administration are therein discussed in all their possible
bearings. Most stress is laid upon the organisation of the communes.

Moderate Republicans observed the movement
with apprehension, and saw in it the one danger
which the Convention had most feared, and
which at that time was designated by the word :
Federation.   To such a morbid height had the
desire for national unity reached in France, that
many Republicans actually preferred the despotic
principle of an administrative centralisation to
the autonomy of the communes. This party perfectly understood Louslalot proposing in 1789
that every commune should not only have the
power of freely regulating its own affairs, but
that this should also be effected without the
intervention of a communal council.   But they
shrank back from the idea of abolishing the
Government as from annihilation. Had not even
Considerant related how, when Rittinghausen
first spoke of a direct government, he listened
to him with amazed incredulity ? The men of
the National, who wanted to maintain the Republic, were opposed to this splitting up of
France into 37,000 deliberative assemblies,

which, as they said, would not in a national
crisis supply the energy and enthusiasm of a
convention. They referred to Montesquieu, who
refuted the demand that the people alone should
make the laws, and who at most had admitted
that a senate, as in Rome and Athens, should
only have the power to pass laws for a year,
which after being sanctioned by the entire people
should be permanently voted. They referred to
Rousseau, who had declared that a true democracy
had never existed, and that the people could only
rule itself if it were composed of gods. It was
easy to understand that the Conservative party
criticised this movement still more sharply than
did the Moderate Republicans. The Conservative
party saw with horror their own disunion, and
against them the close ranks of the Anarchists,
as the opponents of the government machine
called themselves. Thiers said, in warning tones,
in the Legislative Assembly, "Why do we not
all naturally respect one another in the interest
of representative government, *which runs very
great dangers*, and I call heaven and earth to
witness that these dangers arise not by my fault,
or by the excesses which we have committed."

In order perfectly to understand the tragedy
of the *coup d'état*, how a nation could tolerate
an act which robbed it of all its liberty, we must

take the trouble to read the Bonapartist journals of that day. The idea of abolishing the
interest-bearing quality of capital was represented as a conspiracy against property and a
robbery. The proposals for a direct government,
which were equivalent to the abolition of all
government, made it still easier to accuse the
Red Republicans of designing the annihilation
of all education and civilisation. On the other
hand, there were men of the Moderate party who
regarded the tendency of the working class to
abolish the Government as one of the unavoidable questions of the age which could not be
slurred over, but they believed that they could
express its true significance by the formula,
"simplification of the government." Emile de
Girardin was at the head of this movement. In
the last days of August 1848, he went to General
Cavaignac, who at that time having put down the
June insurrection was, as President of the Council of Ministers, at the head of the Government,
and implored him to relinquish the ambition of
being President of the Republic, and to oppose
in the National Assembly a constitution which
should have a President of the Republic. Girardin desired that the then provisional should be
made the definitive form of government. The
President of the Council of Ministers should form

the head of the Government. As long as the majority in the Chamber supported him by their votes, so long he should remain in office; but that the power should at once pass into other hands when the majority withdrew their confidence from him.

M. Grevy, the late President of the National Assembly, brought forward the same proposition in the following amendment, when the draft of the Constitution was being discussed: "The National Assembly transfers the executive power to a citizen, who receives the title of President of the Council of Ministers. He must be a born Frenchman, and at least thirty years of age. The President of the Council of Ministers will be appointed in a secret sitting and by an absolute majority. He will be elected for an unlimited period, but be always removable."

Cavaignac and the majority who were devoted to him opposed this amendment, because they fancied they would always remain in power. Girardin therefore published a pamphlet with the heading, "Why a Constitution?" He wanted the entire French Constitution to be replaced by a simple declaration in ten lines, which could be engraved upon a five-franc piece, and should thus run :—

CONSTITUTION
FRANÇAISE,
1852.

I. La République est la nouvelle forme du gouvernement de la France. II. Tous les droits proclamés par les constitutions antérieures sont reconnus sans discussion, et maintenus sans restrictions. Ils sont inviolables. III. La majorité de la France électorale est représentée par la majorité de l'Assemblée Nationale siégeant en vertu du suffrage direct et universel, et se réunissant de droit le 1er mai de chaque année. IV. Tous les pouvoirs législatifs et exécutifs sont délégués à un président qui reçoit le titre de *Président responsable*. Il est élu par l'Assemblée Nationale ; il choisit et revoque les ministres qu'il s'adjoint. Il exerce ses fonctions aussi longtemps qu'il conserve la confiance de la majorité. Cette confiance s'exprime par un vote spécial et par le vote annuel de recettes et de dépenses de l'État. V. Aucun impôt ne peut être perçu et ne doit être payé s'il n'a pas été voté par l'Assemblée Nationale. V. En cas d'usurpation du pouvoir ou d'atteinte aux libertés publiques, le refus de l'impôt est un droit et un devoir.

Girardin's system was thus based upon the idea of thus making the executive a single power, which should be called "Administrative Power." According to his theory, the President of the Council of Ministers would only have two ministers by his side—one the Minister of Revenue, the other the Minister of Expenditure. Both were to be selected by him. The ministers, on their part, would select and dismiss the directors-general, to whom the separate branches of the administration would be intrusted. Girardin had before his eyes the powerful ministries of Richelieu and Mazarin, to whom France owed so much, and he desired to revive them on a democratic republican footing. This project was based upon an elective and revocable dictatorship, and he held that then no constitution would be necessary.

This outcry against a constitution was by no means a solitary one. Proudhon, who had voted against the National Assembly, declared in a letter to the *Moniteur* that he had opposed it because it was a constitution. He said in this letter: "The existence of a political constitution consists in the separation of the sovereignty, in the partition of authority into two powers, the legislative and executive. This is the principle and the future of every political constitution, since beyond the constitution there is only a sovereign power which issues and executes laws by committees and ministers. I believe that a constitution in a republic is quite superfluous. I hold that the provisional state of affairs which we have had for the last eight months could well be made definitive if a little more regularity were introduced, and a little less respect for monarchical traditions preserved. I am convinced that a constitution, the first act of which consists in the appointment of a president with his privileges and his ambitions, will rather be a danger to, than a guarantee for, liberty."

It was there that Girardin and Proudhon met. Although their systems presented the most marked contradictions, yet both were opposed to

a constitution.   Still in every other party men
had been found antagonistic to a constitution.
Even Cormenin, the President of the Constitution
Committee, had said, " The constitution is too
regulating—too long by a third, perhaps by a
half." In the sitting of the 25th August 1848,
Ledru-Rollin exclaimed : " Constitutions ! We
have in our time so many that we could supply
all the nations of the world with them. What
we want is a social constitution."

These views were held in all the workmen's
clubs. It was concluded that the sovereign
people had no right to prescribe a limit to the
sovereignty of the people, and that every constitution was such a limit. This view was justified
by a comparison of the original draft of the constitution with the second, which was afterwards
adopted. The draft drawn up before the days of
June was a totally different document from that
drawn up while Paris was in a state of siege. Even
in the Absolutist party, whose *arrière-pensée*
was always royalty, there were men who pronounced against any adoption of a constitution.
This party appealed to Le Maistre, who had thus
expressed his ideas : " No constitution emanates
from a deliberation ; the rights of the people are
never written, or if they are, they are only as
simple statements of former unwritten rights.
The more it is written the weaker is the con-

stitution. No nation can give itself liberty if
it has it not. One of the great mistakes of the
age, which comprises all others, was the belief
that a political constitution could.be written and
created *a priori;* whereas reason and experience unite in proving that that which is most
fundamental and essentially constitutional in
the laws of a nation cannot be written. The
veritable English Constitution is that admirable,
unique, and infallible public spirit, beyond all
praise, which directs everything, preserves everything, and saves everything. What is written
is nothing."

While thus men were found in all parties who
either supported a direct government, or the transformation of the government into an administration, or opposed constitutions, there were, on the
other hand, men in the Democratic party itself
who were hostile to the movement. This was
especially the case with Louis Blanc, who expressed himself with passionate severity against
Rittinghausen, Considerant, Ledru-Rollin, and
Proudhon.

Between Louis Blanc and Proudhon a great
gulf existed, across which they could in no way
join hands. Proudhon held that as soon as the
economic revolution was accomplished, government would be a superfluity. Louis Blanc, on
the other hand, considered that the State was the

one thing needful to effect the revolution. He believed that he had thoroughly taken into account the tendency of the workmen towards the abolition of the State by drawing a distinction between the *Etat-maitre* and the *Etat-serviteur*, when he declared that the State, which he held to be necessary, should be only the servant of the people. Proudhon, on the other hand, repudiated the State and the Government because he believed in the personality and autonomy of the masses, and proved that economic reform was identical with the abolition of political masters and representatives.

Proudhon declared that authority emanated from barbarism, and that the State presupposed social antagonism, and was superfluous as soon as strength and weakness no more existed between which the State should step in as mediator.

Louis Blanc, on the other hand, in order to do away with the social antagonism, required the State. It was for him the mould without which no social reform could be produced. A similar split in the Socialistic party in Germany occurred subsequently between Lasalle and Schultze-Delitsch. This antagonism of Proudhon and Louis Blanc could, were it necessary, be further illustrated. It is easy to understand that the former, who began his career by repudiating property and government, and immediately after the

February revolution advocated political enlighten-
ment as the proper aim of mankind, could have
nothing in common with Louis Blanc, whose first
and last thought was the accomplishment of reform by means of the State. Louis Blanc had
always conceived the people as opposed to democracy and continually returning to the authority
of a single man ; consequently he shrank back
from Proudhon's idea of leaving the people to
itself as from a wild phantasy. The controversy
between them was little else than mutual abuse.
It concluded by Proudhon declaring that the
necessary result of economic reform was to put an
end to political institutions and the State, and
that a government would become impossible as
soon as universal suffrage, and therewith the
power of the masses and the consequent subordi-
nation of political power to the will of the people,
had been realised. But Proudhon held that the
idea of the State was entirely founded on the
hypothesis of this impersonality and inaction of
the masses. As soon, however, as these cease,
and capital loses its supremacy, the necessity of
a State for the protection of liberty also ceases.

From this we see the intimate connection in
which workmen's societies, in consequence of
their tendencies directed against capital, could
be used by Proudhon as a weapon and an example for the abolition of the State ; whilst

Louis Blanc would utilise the State for the pur-
pose of breaking the power of capital, and the
workmen's societies to strengthen the power of
the State.

Other weapons were employed by Louis Blanc
against the other Anarchists. In two pamphlets,
headed " Plus de Girondins " and " La Republique une et indivisible," he explained that the
phrase " direct government" meant nothing but
the government of the minority by the majority.
This was indeed a powerful argument against
direct government, because the question, whether in certain cases the majority were justified in coercing the minority, was answered in
the negative. by the democratic Socialist party.
Alfred Bougeart proved, in a pamphlet which
appeared in 1850 (" La Majorité, a-t-elle le Droit
de ramener une Monarchie ? "), that the majority
of the French nation had not the right to re-
establish the monarchy. The Democratic party
had, besides, passed the right of association, the
liberty of speech, and of the press over majorities ; and it was easy for Louis Blanc to prove
that in a direct government the evil of the minority being tyrannised over by the majority
would still exist.   He threatened Ledru-Rollin
with the publication of a certain document, showing that the same Ledru-Rollin who supported
" direct government of the people by the people "

wanted to proclaim his own dictatorship after the February revolution, and had endeavoured to put down Rittinghausen and Considerant by ridicule.

The idea of an entire transformation of the Government thus at this time occupied the attention of all the factions of the Democratic party. As often as elections of members of the Legislative Assembly occurred, questions, the boldness of which seems quite astonishing in the present day, were put to the candidates. Nothing less than the abolition of the entire government machine was discussed.

Numerous pamphlets and newspaper articles detailed how the commune could be made the soul of the State. One of the best writers on this movement was Thoré, who in a striking work proved historically how the Third Estate, when in 1789 it desired to change the order of things, had commenced with a total alteration of the geographical disposition of France. At that time it must have appeared preposterous to the Conservatives suddenly to alter geographical arrangements which had lasted for centuries, and to unite peoples who were not only divided by language, habits, taxes, and even customs-regulations, but who also partially regarded each other as enemies.

Nevertheless, the geographical transformation

of France was rapidly carried out, and Thoré
published a clever plan by which the abolition of
Government could be effected by a simple geographical alteration. At any rate, the plan of
Thoré, which we have not space to describe,
would have utterly broken up the representative
system, although his scheme scarcely went as far
as that of Proudhon, which would have abolished
both the State and the Government.

Proudhon had nothing in common with the
party who desired to introduce direct government. He reproached Rittinghausen and Considerant with not seeing that the same objections
which they levelled against indirect government
could also be brought against direct government.
He showed that as soon as it was admitted that
a community of interests and the progress of
ideas made every kind of government impossible,
direct government would also be impossible; and
thus the matter resolved itself into the question
of government or no government.

Proudhon adroitly proved to the working men
that in all ages the Government, let its origin
have been never so popular, always placed itself
on the side of the richer classes, and against the
lower and more numerous classes; and that
therefore the solution of the social question would
be achieved by clearing away the Government.
He called the history of governments the martyr-

ology of the proletariat, and the working classes
placed themselves on his side. All the workmen's associations thus blended in each other the
political and economic idea, government and
capital; and they regarded being ruled and
misery as one and the same enemy.

We read with astonishment speeches which
were made at that time by workmen, in
which the fact was clearly developed, that, in
accordance with the ideas of Proudhon, the object of Government was to maintain order despite
opposing interests, that it should be in place of
economic order or industrial harmony. The
conclusion of these popular speeches was always,
that as soon as the politico-economical harmony
should be established, Government would be
superfluous and cease of itself. And this was
precisely the standpoint of Proudhon.

Proudhon, in his "Idée générale de la Revolution du 19ᵐᵉ Siècle," diffusely proved how
reciprocity from a national economical point of
view, and contract in a political sense, comprise
the organic principle of the revolution in the
nineteenth century. He not only spoke against
Government and the representative system, but
he desired to substitute the dominion of contracts
in place of legal authority. He said: "That I
may be free, that I may be subject to no other
law but my own, the authority of the vote must

C

be renounced, and farewell must be said to the
decisions of the national representation and to
Government. In one word, everything that is
divine in Government and society must be suppressed, and the edifice must be rebuilt on the
human idea of contract. In fact, if I treat on
any subject with one or more of my fellow-citizens, it is clear that in that case my will alone
is my law, and that I, if I perform my engage-
ments, am my own government. If, therefore,
I conclude the contract which I conclude with a
few individuals with all, if they could all renew
it among themselves, if every group of citizens
—let them be a commune, canton, department,
corporation, or company, formed by such a contract, and regarded as a moral person—could
similarly treat with another group, it would
exactly be as if my will could thus repeat itself
indefinitely. I should then be certain that a law
which thus came into operation at all points of
the Republic, among millions of different initia-
tives, could be nothing else than my law; and
that if such an arrangement could be called a
government, it would be nothing else than my
government. For contract represents liberty; I
am not free so long as I accept the standard of my
rights and of my duties from any other, even if
the other one should call himself the majority of
society. Further, I am not free so long as I am

compelled to have my laws drawn up for me by
some one else, be he the cleverest and most
honest of judges. Finally, I am not free so
long as I am compelled to employ a deputy who
rules me, let him be the most honest of servants.

"Contracts we would place in lieu of laws.
No laws, either voted by a majority or unani-
mously. Let every citizen, every commune or
corporation, make his or its own laws. In place
of political authorities, we should set up economic powers. In place of the former classes of
citizens, nobility, middle class, and proletariat, we
would set up the categories and specialities of the
functions, such as agriculture, trade, commerce,
&c. In place of public authority, we would set
up collective power. In place of standing armies,
we would set up commercial companies. In
place of police, we would set up identity of interests. In place of political, we would set up
economic centralisation. Do you comprehend
this order without officials, this deep intellectual
unity? Oh! you have never known what unity
is. You can only conceive it when harnessed to
a herd of legislators, prefects, procurators-gene-
ral, custom-officers, and gensdarmes. What
you call union or centralisation is nothing but
an eternal chaos which serves as the basis of an
arbitrary and aimless state of things; it is the
anarchy of the social powers which you have

raised as the argument for a despotism which could not exist without this anarchy."

It would take us too long to pursue these ideas further. Every democrat understood that in our century the question was to effect a revolution by the organisation of credit; that words like "democracy" and "popular sovereignty" did not express the Republican principle, but that the revolution meant "sovereignty of the individual." In many working men's circles the question was mooted whether the party of Progress should be allowed to vote or to elect representatives of the people, and if Socialists should not abstain from all voting. The sovereignty of majorities, which forms the apex of democratic institutions, was openly contested, and the autocracy of the single individual was demanded, or, in other words, the absolute liberty which consists in being without any masters or legislators, while democracy, the offspring of monarchical ideas, contented itself with the right of selecting its masters and lawgivers. Many working men therefore repudiated the name of the democratic Socialist party, and called themselves the party of Absolute Liberty. Never before had it been so thoroughly understood that mankind existed by and for man.

There were, therefore, two formulas to which the Proletarians assented both socially and politically. The one was "*abolition de l'exploitation de l'homme par l'homme*," and the ultimate meaning of this formula was the suppression of the fiction of the productivity of capital. The second formula, which the working class regarded as the guiding-star of the social revolution, was "*abolition du gouvernement de l'homme par l'homme*," and its meaning lay in the demand that all political power must come from beneath and not from above, and that the individual was superior to the State. This latter formula signified, further, that universal suffrage should no longer lead to the domination of the majority over the minority; that the universality of the laws must cease; and that laws should only be binding on that party, or fraction of a party, which specially acknowledged them.

Socially the associations were to form alliances among themselves, which would have led to a union, and, politically, into a federation of the various tendencies or social objects. The workman had at last arrived at that point that he neither recognised a master in the workshop nor a ruler in the State, and proclaimed himself an absolutely free and sovereign being. The people understood its mission, and from this standpoint, at one of the workmen's banquets in Paris, these words were uttered : " The revolutionary power, the power of preservation and of progress, is not to-day in the Government, it is not in the Assembly; it is in you. The people alone, acting on itself without any intermediary, can achieve the economic revolution founded in February. The people alone can save civilisation, and cause humanity to advance."

While, therefore, the privileged classes saw civilisation threatened by the proletariat, the disinherited poorer classes hurled back the reproach, and claimed for themselves alone the mission of raising humanity, debased by capital and Government, to true education, liberty, and the enjoyment of life.

CHAPTER II.

THE reader has now a general idea of the task
which the modern Titans who desire to renew the
conflict against Government have set themselves.
The first objection which has been brought against
them from all sides originated in the religious
belief in laws. Many persons are sufficiently
revolutionary to regard the diminution of the
governing power to be possible, but the super-
stitious reverence for a legislative assembly
seems to be ineradicable. Let us for a moment
identify ourselves with the view of the laws held
by the antagonists of the State.

The State has only one life and one existence
—the law. On whichever side of Liberalism we
may stand, so long as we recognise the State in
its inherited form, we shall always see in the
laws the beginning and the end of human society,
the pillars of education, the protection of the
weak, the equalisation of social distinctions, and
the sanctuary of justice.

Revolutionists have hitherto been distin-

guished from reactionists only by the fact that
the former have sought to pass better laws than
the latter, and have taken great pains to make
people happy.   Otherwise there is no difference
between Louis XIV., who made his uncontrolled
will equivalent to law, and therefore said, " I
am the State," and Montesquieu, Rousseau,
Robespierre, St Just, &c.   What the former
arrogated to himself, the latter demanded from
the lawgivers.   Mankind is to them as dough,
which their wisdom would knead; they invent an art to lead men and to make them
happy.   Montesquieu, who even now is quoted
by revolutionists, founded this modern adoration
of the laws, these claims on the wisdom of legislators, this beatification and education by laws,
and this demand for a mechanical sense of
legality.

Laws are everything to him : they are the cows
whose teats mankind should suck ; and he teaches
the legislators what course they are to take with
mankind, even as the farmer instructs his pupils
how to plough the land.   Rousseau also mixes
himself up in everything.   With a veritable rage
for making people happy, he introduces the various plans which legislators should adopt, and
how he should wind up the social machine and
set it going.   He calls the legislator the mechanician who invents the machine.   Mankind

is for him only the passive multitude which is entirely ruled by the lawgiver, of whom he remarks, "He who undertakes to give institutions to a people must feel within himself a power of being able to change human nature, to transform every individual man, to alter the constitution of mankind, to strengthen them; in one word, he must take from mankind their own power and impart to them a foreign power." And to this despot is attributed an influence on the great popular act of the French Revolution !

All the philosophers of the eighteenth century, all the men of the Convention, expected the salvation of society from individual men who should head society, but who yet knew nothing whatever of the life of the masses. The people stood as a lifeless, silent mass before them : society had come to self-consciousness; it palpitated and voted with vital power, while they studied by what means they should impart life to it. A new age had commenced; the Convention wanted to ape that antiquity, wherein one or two men represented the people.

With the complete vanity of authority, St Just said, "The lawgiver commands the future : his business is to wish good; his task to make men as he would have them." The same rage for government gushes through all Robespierre's speeches, which swarm with superficial phrases.

It is really painful to read the speeches of
these men, who in their delusion went so far as
to believe that they could abolish all the vices of
humanity, could they but put mankind in leading strings. The initiative of the people was
unknown to all the politicians of the eighteenth
century.

Every one wanted to carry out his own will,
either to improve, carve, experimentalise on,
equalise, make happy, or be a guardian to
mankind. Each one believed himself to be a
revolutionist because he fulsomely lauded the
Convention—the Convention which knew not that
a people existed; that this people would be free,
would mind its own business, and required no
guardianship: a Convention which only saw in
itself the will and the soul of the nation, placed
itself outside society, and cobbled first here and
then there, and played the lamentable comedy of
Parliamentarism with red caps.

The revolutionary idea of our century is the
right of individuals, the negation of government
and of the law. Nowadays the law is but the
weapon of parties, which each tries to wrest from
the other. It only serves the passions; it is the
means of dominion and of oppression, the child
of injustice and ambition. The law is the last
lurking-place of the faith in authority; we desire not to be governed by any one, but we

submit to an abstraction—the law. Every arbitrary act of tyranny is tolerated, if only it is done by some twist of a law: and then we consider ourselves free. The law is the fetter which holds the spirit in thrall, and whose bonds must be burst. Once the laws were the expression of universal reason, the public conscience, the justice, the mighty bulwark of mankind against barbarism, the school of humanity. Party passion now has polluted the sanctuary, and the sword of the Goddess of Justice serves the governing classes as a weapon wherewith to frighten, to enslave, and to torture the oppressed. Therefore is it that the people only approve the laws against common crimes and in civil matters, and rejoices whenever an acquitting verdict of the jury withdraws in other cases its prey from the terrible fangs of the law and sets it at liberty. The jury system is destined thoroughly to replace the law. Without laws, there is no government; without government, no State, and without the State there is the free human society, which governs itself in a way, indeed, of which neither any of the previously-existing monarchies or republics, but which other associations, or what has hitherto been called a state in the State, can give an idea. The great political struggle which we now see is the strife of parties for the possession of the weapon—law. The rich will not allow to the

necessitous any share in the making of the laws ;
and, on the other hand, every poor devil wants
to be a lawgiver.

This universal struggle to make the laws is
the cause of all the bloodshed which occurs.
Every owner of property hopes that he alone will
be allowed to make the laws, and every starve-
ling shivering in his garret looks with envy and
anger towards the palace of the Legislative
Assembly.   Thus it is that every revolution commences by the people expelling their lawgivers,
by shouting for an extension of the franchise, and
by hoping to find in universal suffrage, which
until the present forms of society are altered is
the chief weapon of the Government, a guarantee
for the stability of the revolution.

Every political party has, therefore, only one
desire—to obtain possession of the legalising
power.   On this every Utopist bases his scheme
for making mankind happy ; every prophet sets
up the twelve tables of the law ; and French
Socialists write no more theories, but issue formulated decrees even as charlatans juggle off
receipts for wonderful cures.   Every class hopes
that when the war is over the law will remain with
it.   The law is to every party leader the mould
into which the raw material is poured and society
modelled.

Only a small knot of free ungovernable men

desires that in the universal struggle for the post of lawgiver, the law itself may be broken up, and that people may no more be made happy or be governed by Act of Parliament, that the will of neither one man nor of an assembly may be binding, and that with the abolition of written laws authority itself may cease to exist, and mankind awake to self-consciousness and morality. To abrogate laws is far more difficult than to pass them. We belong to the laws. Let us strive to belong to ourselves.

Would that every one were the architect of his own fortune, and that leading-strings, rods, and pap should exist only for children, and not for full-grown nations! Would that every one were responsible only for himself, and that it were impossible for the mistakes or malice of a single man, transformed into a law, to be baneful to a whole society!

The more individuals there are, so much higher stands society; but law abolishes all individualism.

We say with pride: " All are equal before the law," instead of crying out with shame: " The law makes us all equal," since it gives us the equality of all wearing the same livery. Robespierre has lamentably said, " Le bonheur est une idée neuve en Europe."

Yes, mankind does not desire freedom. They

struggle against it; they make revolutions to
be governed; they invent democratic schemes to
give a fashion to flunkeyism. Because they are
too cowardly to stand alone, they have invented
the word "nation." Because they shrink from
the thought of an unrestrained individual freedom, they become enthusiastic for a sovereignty
of the people. There is only one liberty, and
that is the sovereignty of each individual. The
so-called sovereignty of the people kills individual liberty as much as does divine right, and is
as mystical and soul-deadening. Every man is
his own lord and lawgiver. The law must not
be poured into us, but must come from out of us.
Democracy, which will soon be as notorious as
aristocracy, has only invented the science of
hammering and welding the fetters upon each
single individual. Universal suffrage has now
no other object than to throw a little mantle of
liberty over the general serfdom. A prison does
not become a temple of liberty because those
words are inscribed above it.

One fights only for the liberties of the people,
but not for the liberty of each individual. Abstract word "people," spectre, shadow, thou
cheatest each separate individual of his liberty !
Mankind, thou robbest the man !

Why should liberty be transformed into the
abstract? Must, then, the despotic State-tie

which holds the entirety together in chains of
liberty exist? Must I, a single individual, by
the foolish abstraction of popular sovereignty be
content with things which I regard as false, and
which drive me back a century? May it not be
allowed for a hundred individuals to band themselves together in unrestrained liberty, while
another hundred continue the old system of
legal guardianship? Away with the notions of
universality! we will not be citizens. As soon
as we adopt this title of democracy, we are once
more the subjects of a mocking spectre called
popular sovereignty. We will be separate individuals, we will be men, we will be unrestrain-
edly free.

True love lies in egotism. As separate individuals, we shall centralise our interests and
form larger combination, just as we voluntarily
form marriage ties. No one shall be dragged
before an altar, and there compelled to say Yes.
Let us gather round the table, and let each one
consume his portion of popular sovereignty. We
will all be sovereigns. Let us give up a system
which only calls us sovereign on the day when
we elect our sovereign and master, on the day
when we are allowed to commit suicide. Awake!
let us no longer be a manufactory for the production of representatives!

A man can as little transfer sovereiguty as he

can get another to live for him. We must, by
the abolition of the Government, come to live for
ourselves. At present all social life is concentrated in the State powers. The separate subjects or citizens are immovable or silent. Their
immovability is called order, a congested condition in which all the blood of the State body
rushes to the head, and forms the harmony of the
State ; but when the blood flows into the separate
veins, and causes them to palpitate, then it is
called anarchy.

Man must be freed from man. Not the will of
another, but only the inner voice of my reason,
can control me. Hitherto the Government has
only been personal ; a single individual or an
assembly could say, " I am the State." Government must be impersonal, or, what is the same
thing, it must disappear. This will be effected
by all great States dissolving and composing a
collection of small federative States, which will
have as little practical government as have now
parishes. As these latter have only administrative but no political officials, and as these
administrative officials can in no way assail the
personal liberty of individuals, even so at some
future time will great States cease to exist, with
their armies, officials, ministers, and all the
other paraphernalia of government. No State
will then be able to have a policy ; men will live

unruled, impose upon themselves laws in smaller
circles, but will not receive general laws from governments or parliaments. In this way the citizens would centralise their interests. Chambers of
commerce, which are established by the free elections of commercial men, would thus, for instance,
represent trade interests, and these chambers
would exercise administrative and judicial functions for the general body. Religious interests,
matters relating to public instruction, public
works, &c., would, without State intervention,
be administered by an understanding of the
parishes among themselves, and the other persons interested in them.

But all parliaments, all legislative institutions,
all political secretiveness with which the millions
of men who compose the State have nothing to
do, would cease to exist. Mankind would thus,
by its more enlightened formation, return again
to the primitive times of the small Greek States.
For the smaller the State the greater would be
the liberty, and the sooner it would be possible
to abolish all government—that is, to transform
it into a simple administration, without political
significance, and to make it possible for each
individual to take part in public affairs.

D

CHAPTER III.

THE idea of the abolition of the State was most profoundly explained by Proudhon, whose system is based not only on political motives, but also politico-economical reasons; and we shall therefore take him as an illustrative example, although we could find similar examples in Spain, Germany, Switzerland, Italy, and even in Russia. Since his death his name has been less prominent. There was, however, a time when his banner was considered in France as synonymous with a social cataclysm; and the horrors of the Commune in Paris are even now attributed to the misunderstanding of his ideas.

Proudhon is the philosopher of the French Revolution of 1848; and as the ancients carried with them their bards into the battle, so he, the dreamer, accompanies the revolutionary combatants and rejoices in their work. In June 1848, while on all sides the battle was raging, he stood on one of the bridges, and being asked by a representative what he was doing there, replied, as he pointed to the cannon-balls hurling through

the air and the burning house, that he was gazing on the sublime and dreadful play. This
circumstance has, it is true, been denied; but
those who knew Proudhon best firmly believe it,
so characteristic is it of the man. If true, his
feelings as he there stood must have been those
of an astronomer, who having prophesied the
destruction of the world, sees the fulfilment of
his prediction commenced.

Proudhon calculated misery, and knew exactly
how long the patience of hunger would endure.
He reduced the entire social criticism to a system
of double-entry. In all his later writings he
keeps a formal account of the economic relations
of society, and proves by figures how the bal-
ance may be upset, and at what particular point
the deficit will be discovered. In his later writings he abandoned his first revolutionary haste,
and the impetuosity of his earlier works. He
who once begins to calculate is quiet.

In gambling-houses, amidst the passionately
excited crowd, men are often seen, who have
already lost all they possess, silently smiling,
and pricking in on their cards the winning num-
bers, as if the mere fact of watching the varying
chances of the game in which they can only take
a spectator's part had a calming influence upon
their over-excited brains. For hours they will
thus tranquilly sit and calculate, while by their

sides each minute estates and fortunes are being
lost, and the victims of ill fortune are franti-
cally rushing away from the scene of their mis-
fortunes. So sat Proudhon in the Conciergerie,
whither his revolutionary doctrines had brought
him, and coldly worked out the social problem.

He became the book-keeper of human misery.
With frightful calmness his figures told him
what particular units of humanity would starve.
In one of his many pamphlets he reduced the
relations of the labourer to the capitalist to a
mathematical formula, and brought out the result
thus : "The work of the labourers B to L for the
capitalist equals 10, and their consumption only
9 ; in other words, the capitalist has eaten one
labourer."

On another occasion he said, " For nearly ten
years I have not ceased calling out to property,
'Thou art the god not only of murder, but of
suicide ;' and in return the capitalists, half
ruined, and the sophists cry, 'Down with him !'
But 'Down with him !' means, in times of
revolution, 'Strike him dead !' Come now, you
journalists of property ; come, theologians with
the biblical jargon ; philosophers, moralists,
jurists, publicists, ideologists, with your mystical gibberish ; economists with the double
tongue, and if you will kill me with the first
salvo, I will say to you with my last breath,

'Before you speak of property, go, all of you, to M. Hippolyte Vannier, 15 Rue de Rambuteau, and take a lesson in book-keeping. Until then you are all only liars and cowards.'"

This is quite the obstinate tone of a book-keeper whose accounts are contested. Such a reply might an astrologer, who from his observation of the heavenly bodies had calculated the future, have given to one who doubted the accuracy of the horoscope. Just as obscurely does he cry aloud to his friends in his " Confessions d'un Revolutionnaire," " Study a revolution. Learn to comprehend it." Like an augur he examines the entrails, and from them foretells what is to come.

In the camp of the Economists stands the mysterious form of Malthus calculating the necessity of misery ; and in the opposite camp of the Socialists stands Proudhon, and calculates to the labourers whence comes starvation. Malthus, in gloomy resignation, closes his book and says, " The guests on earth exceed the number of plates laid for them, and there is no remedy against starvation."

Proudhon was the mathematical antagonist of Malthus ; he introduces other elements in his calculations, and arrives at other results. Malthus began to calculate during the first French Revolution, and was scared by the bloodshed ;.

and Proudhon continued the calculations during
the revolution of February. Both are hermits
amidst the crowd of the age ; and as Archimedes
cried out to the invading soldiers, "Do not
touch my circle," so they stand brooding apart
from the combatants, and each believes himself
to have solved the problem of society.

Proudhon stands tragically and completely
apart from his age. His pathos cannot be
doubted ; we can never for an instant question
that it is fire which burns within him. Every firm
conviction is a species of madness ; and in Proudhon's every word the intensest conviction is present. Every sentence comes from his soul, and
we even seem to see his fiery breath. Once he
wrote, " The writer of these lines must believe
that at this moment the world is mad." He
concluded another of his peculiar desponding
articles with the following words : " Accursed
be my cotemporaries. Only those minds who do
not understand the unhappiness and the loneliness of my genius can mistake these sharp words.
Unspoken they are the culminating points of
every soul—which negates."

He stands amidst ruins and rejoices. He lies
down amidst the corpses of the age in order that
he may revel in the full flood of life within him.
He is the Nero of literature, who sings whilst the
great fire is burning. He places as a motto to

one of his books, " Levabo ad cœlum manum
meam et dicam vivo ego in æternum." Proudhon feels in his veins the life-blood of the next
century, therefore he shouts aloud as one
drunken with vitality. He is Lot escaping
from the doomed Sodom. Proudhon is the revolution embodied and conscious of its own wants :
in him revolution for the first time found its
logic. He meets us with a cold incisive logic, a
guillotine of words, a Bastille-storming, fear-
inspiring logic ; a logic before which lord high
chamberlains tremble ; a logic from which capital
finds no lurking-places ; a logic which tears away
the shirt from modern society, and which washes
off the paint. His speech is of the revolution—
bold, hasty, overwhelming, crushing, lightning
and thunder in one. Proudhon is a German
Frenchman. He writes with a deep-thinking
German intellect, and a French power of execution. There is something of the Puritan element in
his development. One sees in him the sword and
the Bible, while ever and anon the upstart, the
self-educated man, is present.

Proudhon annihilated all authority ; he reduces
the State to its component parts ; he leads capital back to his starting-point ; he kills money by
its own mother—barter ; he compels the power of
the people to take the initiative ; he destroys the
right to be idle ; he storms heaven and trans-

forms earth. He was to be feared. We might love him or we might hate him, but no one could laugh at him. When he read his financial scheme to the Constituent Assembly, and it was received with general laughter, he said coldly, standing placidly amidst the unexampled tumult raging around him, " Citizens, I regret that my words should so excite your laughter, since that which I say will kill you."

In those words rang out from the tribune, for the first time in the history of the educated world, the sharp voice of the proletariat, clearly and precisely, addressing its demands to society. Then it was that Proudhon felt his mission; and when he was interrupted by a question as to whom his speech was addressed, he replied, " Since I use the two pronouns ' we' and ' you,' it is clear that at this moment I personify myself with the proletariat, and you with the middle class."

Thus Proudhon placed himself outside the pale of society, and at war with it. Inexorably he pointed out the social contradictions he had in view, when on this occasion he declared, " The income-tax is called a robbery : what shall we say to the taxation of labour? That can only be called murder." Thereupon he began to calculate. He calculated the economy of society, and he calculated until the Assembly was frightened. And as a tyrant drowns by beat of drum

the last words of one condemned to death, so did
the members drown his voice by tumultuous
noises, and prevent him finishing his speech.
But in vain. Proudhon's voice grew ever louder
and louder ; his speech was firm and distinct,
and his words sound further and farther, and
will yet be long heard.

When Proudhon was a prisoner in the Conciergerie, the upper and middle classes read the
pamphlets and newspapers he issued from his cell.
They looked upon him as one looks upon a wild
beast in a cage. He affected, in order to obtain
a hearing, the air of one who wished to confess
his sins, and he called his work " The Confessions of a Revolutionist;" and we might have
believed we were about to hear the words of a
penitent sinner when he commenced with these
words, " I will explain the motives of all my
actions, and confess all my faults ; and if in so
doing a bold word, a hasty thought, should
escape my pen, pardon me as you would a
humbled sinner."

With these words he entered the confessional,
and then shrieked out the most horrible tales
into the ears of his father-confessor. Who was
this man who thus affrighted the French middle
class ? A short review of his writings will tell
us who he was.

In his controversy with Louis Blanc, he de-

clared that the Revolution of the nineteenth century had a twofold object. Economically, the
first object was the amalgamation of the labourer
and the capitalist by the democratisation of credit, the annihilation of interest on capital, and
the transformation of all commercial transactions which have for their object the means of
labour and production. In this connection there
only existed two parties in France—that of
labour and of capital. Politically, the second
object was to merge the State in society—*i.e.*,
the cessation of all authority, and the suppression of the entire machinery of Government by
the abolition of taxation, the simplification of
the administrative arrangements, or, in other
words, by the organisation of universal suffrage.
From this point of view he saw in France only
two parties—the party of liberty and the party
of Government. Proudhon, therefore, laid down
the following proposition as the formula of his
political and economical system : Abolition of the
economical exhaustion of man by man, and abolition of the government of man by man. In
this double direction run all the propositions of
Proudhon : on the one side, towards the abolition of interest and the introduction of gratuitous
credit ; on the other side, towards the suppression of taxation, and, as a natural corollary, the
extinction of Government.

According to his views, the abolition of State and capital depends each upon the other. What in politics is called authority is analogous and equivalent to what in political economy is called property. Proudhon can only express the revolutionary idea in its simplicity and grandeur by the word anarchy: for nations in their nonage, chaos and nothingness; for full-grown peoples, life and light.

This double object of his writings, as well as his attitude towards the socialist development of France, are most glowingly, passionately, and despairingly described by Proudhon himself in his above-mentioned "Confessions d'un Revolutionnaire pour servir d'Histoire de la Revolution de Février." He wrote this work in the Conciergerie. It is the writing of a prisoner who holds himself freer than any other person; a victorious shout from one vanquished. He commenced the gloomy diary which he wrote on the walls of his cell with the words : " For the last four months I have observed their triumph, these charlatans of family and property. My eye follows their drunken movements, and at every look, every word that escapes them, I say, ' They are lost.' In the bitterness of my soul I will speak to my fellow-citizens. Hear the rebellion of a man who once deceived himself, but who yet was ever true to mankind. May my voice pene-

trate your ears as the voice of one condemned, as
the conscience of a prison."

Proudhon had the destructive power and the
solitude of fire. Fire consorts with nothing but
itself, and can only extend itself by destruction.
How great and fearful is the working of the
flame ! how it eats through wood and iron !
What influence has the doctrine of Proudhon
had upon the development of affairs in France !
How has he rooted up the tyranny of reaction,
and himself in turn tyrannised over his party !
From the very commencement of the February
revolution, Proudhon in his paper was constantly
in advance of all the other Socialistic journals,
even of the Mountaineers in the National
Assembly, and continually compelled them to
follow his lead against their will. The barri-
cades of February were scarcely cleared away,
every one was entangled in the vortex of the
revolution, when he began his independent course
of organisation. Every rival preaching Socialism
was attacked by him, and he beat them down in
order that he might continue the fight alone. The
Fourierist school, with Considerant at its head,
was annihilated by him ; the utter emptiness of
Pierre Leroux and the chimerical tendencies of
Louis Blanc were equally demolished by him. No
one castigated the Provisional Government so
unmercifully as he. In him the Mountain found

its sharpest critic. The Mountain, which at
their banquet of the 22d September 1848 had
spoken so energetically against Socialism,
adopted suddenly, and chiefly in consequence of
his compulsion, the social Democratic Republic
as its banner. Similarly the ideas of free credit,
a bank of exchange, the abolition of all government, were adopted chiefly through his instru-
mentality. The union of the proletariat and the
middle class was first preached by him despite
the abyss which separated them, and which party
hatred sought daily to widen. He it was who
first urged the Democratic party constitutionally
to oppose the reaction, and he did it in those
gloomy days when the ardent Revolutionists regarded him as one whose doctrines would act as
oil upon the troubled waters of the time.

Proudhon had an amount of polemical power
seldom possessed by genius. Like vitriol, he ate
away modern society, he dissolved every hin-
drance. Once he called Socialism a protest, a
very vague, but for him very significant, declaration. Proudhon would take the initiative; he
could enter into controversy with his own
scholars, ay, even with himself. History is to
him the extrusion of one Utopia by another.
Official Utopias, realisable for a moment, but
which have no true life, will continually be opposed by other Utopias—for the most part pure

impossibilities, or possibilities practicable only
up to a certain point—and thus by this constant
course of dissolution and destruction mankind
progresses. Such Utopias, which undermine
existing conditions, apparently possessing a
reality, but which are yet utterly Utopian, must
incessantly crop up in history. The Utopias
of Pythagoras, Plato, the Manichæans, Albigen-
ses, Hussites, Anabaptists, of Campanella, Sir
Thomas More, De Morelly, and Babœuf, join
hands in succession. The Utopias bring inter-
mixture and syntheses into society, and cause
mankind to recognise their contradictions. Yet
every Utopia, when it has exhausted the power
which gave it being, must be refuted.

Proudhon comes forward as the destroyer of
all Utopias. His war-cry is, "Destruam et
ædificabo;" and he translates this biblical
sentence by the words, "I destroy, *therefore* I
build up."

Proudhon recognises two species of Utopia,
both of which he equally combats : firstly, the
one which seeks to achieve everything by a
single man, and which he calls Economicism ;
and, secondly, the other, which seeks to effect
everything by society, and which he calls Socialism, and more often Communism. This dialectic form was retained by him in all his
writings, and was most clearly apparent in his

chief work, " Contradictions." Proudhon therefore wages war against all economists, and also
against all socialists. The only justification of
the social Utopias which he recognises, is so far
as it is a protest, against official Utopias. One
of the chief points, therefore, of Proudhon's doctrine is naturally a criticism of our entire economic
edifice, which rests upon a hypothesis, a fiction,
in fact, upon a Utopia—viz., the productiveness
of capital. In consequence of this hypothesis,
one-half of the products of society flows out of
the hands of the working classes, under the
names of rent, hire, contract, agio or interest,
into those of the capitalists, proprietors, and
contractors.

This condition is the official Utopia which
must be dissolved by the social Utopias of St
Simon, Fourier, Cabet, Louis Blanc, and Pierre
Leroux. That done, its part is played, and
Proudhon then demands the entire arena for
liberty. This two-edged sword was constantly
wielded by him as a weapon. While on the one
hand he sweeps away the dead national economy,
on the other he roots out Socialism, which would
enter upon the inheritance.

Proudhon would have perfect liberty : he took
it by storm. When a prisoner in the Conciergerie, and later in Doullens, he was the first
man in France. Proudhon fought for political

and social liberty: this is his general characteristic.   Politically there is no freedom for him as
long as a government at all exists, and socially
he only feels himself free when feudal property
and capital vanish.   On another occasion, which
we shall explain later, this latter tendency was
carried out in a sense diametrically opposed to
Communism.   According to his views, citizen is
only then free when the State ceases ; and so
long as capital exists, so long does the labourer
remain a slave.

Hegel in Germany produced Feuerbach, and
in France Proudhon ; and as Proudhon owes to
him his dialectic form, so also did he found his
metaphysical ideas, which must here be intro-
ductorily glanced at, upon Hegel's doctrine.

To him God is eternal, man progressive reason.   Each is requisite to the other, and both
complete each another.   Proudhon regards this
harmony as the government of Providence.   This
harmony is proverbially expressed by the sentence, " Help yourself, and God will help you."
In his metaphysical views, he follows the forma-
listic course of Kant.   To him it is clear that
no investigation into the being of God can lead
to any result, and he pursues, therefore, only
" The Biography of the Idea of God."   He ana-
lyses the belief in God, and thereby breaks the
spell which makes the idea inaccessible to rea-

son. God is thus transformed into his own ideal, into humanity. The theological dogma no longer remains the mystery of the Infinite, but is the law of our collective and individual liberty. Humanity contemplates itself, and calls the picture God. Religion and society are synonymous.

Holding these metaphysical views, Proudhon was in France accused of being an atheist. As he once related in his " Voix du Peuple," letters were sent to him with the address, " M. Proudhon, the personal enemy of God." Notwithstanding this, Proudhon on many occasions denounced materialist atheism, and compared it to suicide.

Proudhon is not always original in his range of ideas. His antagonists even contended that he had no originality, and ascribed the well-known saying, " *La propriété c'est le vol*," to Brissot. Still, what is always original in him is the form of his intellectual productions. He plunges every thought into the Revolution, and imparts to each of his sentences a violent crushing character. He appears always fighting and never debating ; so that with him everything appeared new and also was new. He saw the sober British idea of self-government, which constitutional doctrinaires preached uncontrolledly in absolute States, and while he discussed it, evolved therefrom the most revolutionary ideas—the abolition of Government, the extinction of the State.

Proudhon was the atheist of politics. His atheism was not that of the eighteenth century, but rather a more concrete, more sensual atheism, which looked not to the empty heaven but to the teeming earth ; an atheism that did not despair because it only had the earth, but would precisely have nothing but the earth ; an atheism which, while it allowed no domination to God, would also have no more government of men.

Similarly Proudhon criticised in all his writings the principle, the object, and the right of government, and came to the conclusion that philosophy could as little prove the existence of a government as of a God. For him, government, like God, is not an object of knowledge but of faith. He asks, " Why do we believe in a government ? Whence comes the idea of authority in human society ? this fiction of a superior being called ' State ' ! Ought it not to be with the Government as with God and the Absolutists, which have so long and fruitlessly engaged the attention of philosophers ? And as we have already, by means of philosophical analysis, found, in reference to God and religion, that mankind beneath the allegory of its religious myths was but pursuing its own ideal, could we not also seek what they desire by the allegory of their political myths?" The political arrangements, so varying and contradictory, are not, according to his ideas, material for society, but appear rather as simple formulas and hypothetical combinations, by means of which civilisation maintains an appearance of order, or, to speak more correctly, seeks order.

Instead, therefore, of seeing in Government the organ and expression of society as held by the Absolutists, the instrument of order according to doctrinaire ideas, the means of revolution, the belief of the Radicals, Proudhon only recognised in it a phenomenon of social life, the external representation of our rights, the development of one of our capabilities.

Proudhon further proclaimed that government, like religion, was a manifestation of social spontaneity. What humanity seeks in religion, and calls God, is itself; and what the citizen seeks in government, and calls either king, emperor, or president, is freedom.

The best form of government, as the best religion, literally accepted, is a contradictory idea. The question is not in the least how we shall be best governed, but how we shall be freest. Government of man by man is as little to be permitted as the economical exhaustion of one man by another. That was one of the chief formulas of Proudhon.

So consistent is Proudhon, that he only recognises as a Republic that land where the people exist without representation or magistracy; and he calls every one a monarchist who does not strive to achieve the suppression of all government—*i.e.*, anarchy. He holds that whoever admits the economic revolution proclaims thereby the cessation of the State. This abolition of the State is, he declares, the necessary consequence of the organisation of credit and the reform of taxation, since by this double innovation government will be gradually superfluous and impossible.

Government stands just on the same footing as feudal property, as loans or interest, as absolute or constitutional monarchy, as judicial institutions, &c., which have all served as an education for liberty, but which fall and become powerless as soon as liberty has reached its full growth. In his work, " Confessions of a Revolutionist," this feeling is most aggressively expressed. He says : " All men are free and equal; therefore is society, in accordance with its nature and destiny, autonomic and ungovernable. As every one's circle of activity is fixed by the natural division of labour, and the choice of a condition of life which each one finds in due course, so are the social functions combined in such a manner that they must harmoniously co-operate.

Order springs from the free activity of all : there is no government. Whoso lays a hand upon me to govern me is a usurper and a tyrant. I declare him my enemy."

He was asked : " Then you would abolish Government ? You would have no constitution ? Who, then, would maintain order in society ? What would you have in place of the State, in place of the police, in place of the great political powers ?" He replied : " Nothing. Society is perpetual motion. It does not require to be wound up, and it is unnecessary to beat time for it. It has in itself its pendulum, and its spring is always wound up. An organised society needs laws as little as lawgivers. Laws are in society as a spider's web in a beehive. They only serve to catch the bees."

Proudhon declared that society could only be regarded as organised when no longer any one existed to make or observe laws, or to live in accordance with them. It was only because society had up to the present time never been organised, and had always found itself in course of organisation, that lawgivers, statesmen, heroes, and policemen had been necessary.

Starting with this view of government, Proudhon laid down a totally different definition of Monarchy and Republicanism to that laid down by the general run of Republicans, who believe that

society can be republicanised by simply expelling
the king.   To him Monarchy is not an individual,
a family, an incarnation of popular sovereignty,
but a faith and a system : a faith in a divine
right and a system of government.   Both elements he found as deeply rooted in the Democrats as in the Royalists.

CHAPTER IV.

PROUDHON thus proved to the Republicans that
they had no idea of what a government consisted : " Monarchy is not one of those things
which vanish with the first breath, or by a decree
of the Hotel de Ville.' To change society from
a monarchy to a republic is as difficult as to
transform the human mind. Centuries, the work
of twenty generations, are needed to reach the
goal. You believe when you lost the Emperor,
or later when you drove out Charles X. or Louis
Philippe, that you had destroyed this institution,
whereas you had but taken down the signboard.
The system is inviolate in your ideas and habits.
I should astonish many an honest democrat if
I undertook to prove to him that he and the
whole Democratic party have never held any but
monarchical ideas, that everything they think,
speak, propose, or dream of is monarchy. The
Communism of the Icarians, what is it but absolute monarchy? Even so is it with the other
social Utopias. To found liberty, equality, and
fraternity, Cabet makes himself a king, Saint

Simon a high priest, Pierre Leroux a prophet, and Louis Blanc a dictator. The most insignificant manager of a working men's association strives to gather all the working men of his station beneath his hand. There is always the same hierarchical prejudice, the same mania for government. Superstition in that which should emanate from divine right is, spite of all the calumnies of which it has been the object, more deeply rooted than ever. As, according to a thoroughly monarchical proverb, ' the voice of the people is the voice of God,' so is divine right nothing more than a national decree formulated by universal suffrage. Without going back to the election of Hugh Capet, not mentioning the equally wonderful election of Louis Buonaparte as President of the Republic, yet the species of sanctification which the representatives of the people receive in the sacrament of popular election is of this a proof. In what, I ask, does the representative of the people elected by universal suffrage differ from a divine-right monarch? The representative concentrates in his person the will, the being of one hundred thousand, perhaps two hundred thousand, perhaps a million citizens of the State. He is invested with unlimited, absolute, full powers. He is able to pass laws on, to decide, to regulate all divine and human, natural and supernatural,

affairs in his complete authority, or, as is said
of the Pope, without previous study, and only
in consequence of the knowledge imparted to
him by the act of election. The constitution
declares him to be inviolable, his decrees are
infallible. What can the man-king, the only
representative of sovereignty, do more than this?
The man, elected by four departments at once,
is by this simple fact of the accumulation of
votes an extraordinary personage ; and when
more than five millions of votes are recorded
for him, a god! Hence the people conceives
for those whom it has elected an absolute adoration ; and what is really laughable, this idolatry
for representatives seizes also those persons who
are the objects of the idolatry. Look at these
men who majestically have encamped upon the
Parliamentary Sinai, there is not one of them
but arrogates to himself a species of jurisdiction
over the thoughts of the people. If the 450
members of the Legislative majority are so well
leading us on, that is only because they believe
themselves to be more infallible, more legitimate, more king than Carl X. or Louis
Philippe. The monarchical principle is as quick,
as complete in an assembly emanating from the
entrails of a people as in a legitimate king: it
will be regarded as infallible, and will be treated
with as much majesty as the more or less authen-

tic scion of a family privileged and sanctified *ad hoc.* The true divine right is universal suffrage, according as we exercise it."

Proudhon regards the State as the external constitution of social power. By this external constitution of its power and sovereignty, the people does not govern itself, but soon either au individual, or several persons, are by the title of election or inheritance empowered to rule. The people is thus regarded as incompetent to govern itself, and we start with the hypothesis that society can only express itself in the monarchical incarnation, the aristocratic usurpation, or the democratic mandate.

Proudhon denies this conception of a collective being, the State, the Government, whether it adopts a royalist or a democratic colouring, and demands the personage, the autonomy, the physical, intellectual, and moral individuality of the masses. He is of opinion that every State constitution has no other object than to lead society to this condition of autonomy, and that absolute monarchy, as well as representative democracy, are but rungs of the political ladder on which societies rise to a knowledge and possession of themselves. In this anarchy he recognises the highest degree of liberty and order mankind can achieve, and the true formula of the Republic, so that between Republic and Government, between

Universal Suffrage and the State, there exists a contradiction.

This view he defends in a double way, first by the historical and negative method, since he proves that every government has become impossible, and that by its very principles a government must be counter-revolutionary and reactionary; and also by the proof that by economic reform and industrial solidarity a people is brought to reflection, and acquires a knowledge of itself, and acts as one individual. And as the psychology of a single individual is investigated, so Proudhon regarded the psychology of nations and humanity as a possible science. Thus Proudhon regards, as the aim of the Revolution which was commenced by the events of February, the establishment of absolute human and civic liberty. With this object he lays down politically the following formula: " Organisation of universal suffrage, and the gradual inversion of the governing power in society;" economically, organisation of circulation and credit—that is, the merging of the capitalist in the workman. This formula forms the starting point of his system, and serves also as a real and direct explanation of the Revolution.

These views on government were first pronounced by Proudhon in 1840, in his work, " What is Property ? or, Inquiries into the Principle of

Right and Government." In the last chapter
of that work the following passage occurs :—

" Which form of government shall we prefer ?
How can you ask ? doubtless answers many
of my young readers; you are a Republican !
Republican, yes; but that word denotes nothing.
Res publica—that is, the public affairs ; so that
every one who will promote public affairs can
call himself a republican. Kings may be con-
sidered as republicans. Well, then, you are a
Democrat ? No ! How? You are a Monarchist ?
No ! A Constitutionalist ? Heaven forbid !
Then you are an Aristocrat ? You want a
mixed system of government? Still less.
What are you, then? I am an Anarchist ! "

This view of the State pervades all his writings, and he confirmed it in his Parliamentary
course. On the 4th November 1848 he addressed a letter to the editor of the *Moniteur*, in
which he explained his vote against the Constitution. He said that after four months' discussion
he found it impossible to abstain from partici-
pating in the vote, but that he considered it
necessary to give an account of his vote. He
did not vote against the Constitution from an
empty mania for opposition or revolutionary
agitation, nor yet because it contained matters
which he much wished away, and did not con-
tain other matters which he should liked to have

seen in it. If such arguments could move the
mind of a representative, there would never be
a vote about a law. He had voted against the
Constitution because it was a constitution. What
constituted a constitution—he refers to a political
constitution, since no other can come in question—was the partition of sovereignty, the separation of power into legislative and executive.
In that consisted the principle and substance of
every constitution ; beyond that there was no
such thing as a constitution—only a sovereign
authority issuing decrees, which were executed
by its committees and ministers. We are unaccustomed to such an organisation of sovereignty,
and yet a republican government is nothing
else. Proudhon held that in a republic a constitution was superfluous, and that the provisional
state of things which had been a power for the
previous eight months, could be made definitive
with somewhat more regularity and somewhat
less respect for monarchical traditions. He was
convinced that the Constitution, the first act of
which consisted in the establishment of a Presidency, with all its prerogatives, ambitions, and
fallacious hopes, was rather a danger to than a
guarantee of liberty. What Proudhon in his
quality of representative carefully expressed in
his letter, that he consistently elaborated in his
writings, not in blind opposition to the necessary

restraints and forms, but in full consciousness of liberty.

This phase of Proudhon's doctrine is for us who have hitherto lived too much in abstract ideas at first confusing and incomprehensible. Our State is practically only an abstract formula, which can only exist as the unnatural and unreal separation of soul and matter. It is only a spiritualistic lie, and contains just as much truth as the immaculate conception of. Mary. At present the question is to pass from the abstract to the real, and that will be effected by the social reform for which Proudhon paved the way. First of all it will fix the relation of man to man, which hitherto has been done by politicians only so far as the most pressing necessity demanded. Up to the present the State has concerned itself about the individual only so far as to give him alms or to throw him into a prison. We now only exist for the State, and not the State for us. Therefore it is impossible to draw a conclusion from State affairs to the condition of its component individual parts, either economically or politically.

Statistics of a State can prove its prosperity by the clearest figures; we can from these figures come to the conclusion that every branch of industry, trade, and agriculture is in the most flourishing condition, and yet it may not be

true. The total amount might not be reducible
to separate amounts, and despite the figures,
two-thirds of the people in the State may be
beggars. National economy has at present treated
all these questions in the lump, it has reflected
only the total amount. So is it politically. A
State as a State can offer the highest amount
of political freedom, and yet no conclusion as to
individual freedom can be drawn. The example
of England will exactly prove this. That State
is nothing but a political formula. The demands
of individual political freedom are there com-
plied with as in no other country, and yet the
individual is not really free.

Mankind can and will be governed no longer.
Proudhon rooted up the State, that Moloch which
consumes us all, sucks our strength, practises
usury with every one, is held together by blood,
and prides itself upon it, and is necessarily based
upon the stupidity of the people.

The good the State has done to mankind is
not to be ascribed to it, but to the social ties
existing in it, from that of family to that of
science. Those individuals alone are great who
have cut themselves loose from the State, who
do not regard the accidental geographical frontier
of the State as a form of mankind, and who only
consider the relationship of their own individuality to that of their fellow-creatures to be

bounded by the universe, and who, driven by a divine egotism, are, like Schiller's Marquis Posa, citizens of an age which is still to come.

The true human individual finds no place in the State, he can call no place in it his home, and feels himself as in the nursery, ruled by the fears of bogies and the rod. State apparatus is antiquated ; mankind will no longer be governed, and will pay no more government taxes. The fearfully tragic side of the State has been long since symbolised in the antique tragedies. Shakespeare represented the madness of royalty and the disintegration of the State; and in the classical masterpiece of Hebbel, "Herodes and Marianne," the contradiction attaching to a kingdom as such, and how thereby every royal person, even the noblest, is morally annihilated, is artistically delineated.

But every kingdom is royal, and every State a kingdom. The form of State is strong, iron, oppressive ; it kills the individual, and is incompatible with liberty. Every one of us digs himself out; we are all under the heap. The State has been for us as has been the mother's body for the embryo ; now mankind frees itself from it. Only by an aberration of reason will government be retained.

To Proudhon belongs the merit of having pointed out to us the way to abolish the State and to organise anarchy. The first words he spoke to society sounded from a small provincial town, and penetrated to the Sorbonne at Paris. They were these, " Property is robbery." With this bitter warning he began his public life. It was to Blanqui senior, the Professor of Economic Science, who from his pulpit in Paris defended modern society, that he spoke these enigmatical and often misinterpreted words.

Prior to this work on property he had published a pamphlet on the celebration of the Sabbath. In this, however, he did not thunder forth in his later and more violent style, but ever and anon he would throw aside his theological cloak which he wore to compete for the prize offered by the Academy of Besançon, and we see his naked form. Once, as if he were softly talking to himself, while speaking of quite other subjects, this sentence escaped him, " Property has not yet had its martyrs; it is the last of the false gods." These words are hidden amidst reflections on Moses and the celebration of the Sabbath. They stand there as a wolf in the sheepfold.

When Proudhon came to Paris, he was so poor that he performed the entire journey from Besançon on foot, not having money enough to pay for a seat even in the poorest conveyance; he brought nothing with him but a definition. He

F

had invented a definition of property analysing
the foundation of society.   And in this formula
he pointed out the entire change which property
had undergone since the commencement of commercial intercourse and credit ; and by so doing
he at the same time so clearly showed the one
great change society had undergone, and also
discovered, as it were, the pin around which the
thread of the future must be wound.   With this
definition he so sharpened the social thought of
the age that with it he could not but inflict
wounds.

So harshly, in so concentrated a manner, did
he express his definition of property, that he
irritated and gave occasion to many misunder-
standings. He, the great opponent of Communism, laid himself open, by his definition of
"property is robbery," to the charge of being
a Communist.   And yet Proudhon had never
attacked property, so far as it was the product
of toil, invention, or labour ; but he showed that
it only possessed value so far as it entered into
the circle of exchange.   In his definition, however, he had in view only the feudal form of property, an object which without any exertion of
its owner brings to that owner interest or rent.
In this definition he found the spell which must
open the door to the social revolution ; in this
definition the great plot of ancient society was

laid bare. It was the declaration of war which
the advancing February revolution sent on before it. It was the eye of Socialism, the justification of reform, the first word of the coming
age, the first Republican thought.

Proudhon knew, too, what point he gave to the
coming revolution by his declaration. He said:
" The definition of property is mine, and it is my
whole ambition to prove that I have understood
its meaning and scope. Property is robbery.
A thousand years hence such a word will never
be spoken twice. I have no other estate on earth
but this definition of property, but to my think-
ing it is more valuable than the millions of
Rothschild, and I venture to say that it will be
the most important event in the reign of Louis
Philippe."

This pride in the new formula proves that in
it the Revolution already raised its head, and the
monopoly of capital as well as the principle of
government were disintegrated.

He called property robbery, because in its
present form the idea of reciprocity is wanting;
and he could, although he was the greatest
opponent of Communism, yet speak of an abolition of property, because he deprived it of its
sting, and only allowed it to exist without it,
just as a man no longer exists as a man when
deprived of his manhood.

Proudhon's abolition of property was only a progressive abolition of interest on capital, without expropriation or the slightest Communistic tendency. If under the word property the right of enjoying the full benefit of one's own labour is understood, he only abolishes false to reinstate true property. Usury is equally only naked property, capital unveiled, the torch held up to society. All property is usurious, there is no property in circulation but has a usurious advantage. Every proprietor is a usurer, ay, even against his will; and this usury of property Proudhon called a robbery.

In his definition of property lay his whole criticism of society, which at one and the same moment inflicts a wound and heals it. Proudhon's criticism of society served to allot to property its place in the economic series, beyond which it is incomprehensible. In his two first works on property he criticised the conception of it by antithesis, and sought to attack its present feudal form by the contradictions which, he pointed out, lay in its very nature.

CHAPTER V.

But it was only first in his *chef-d'œuvre*,
" The Philosophy of Misery," that he entered
upon the path which could lead to a synthetic
solution. He sought out the analogous and
adequate phenomena under which property was
ranged, in order to investigate its nature and its
economical relations. Apart from these relations, property appeared, by the logical construc-
tions in which Proudhon placed it, as a separate
fact, a solitary idea, and therefore incomprehensible and unproductive. But if property
assumes its true form, and be treated within its
own range as a harmonious whole, it loses its
negative specialities.

To arrive at this comprehension of property,
to the idea of social order, he first lays down the
series of contradictions of which property forms
a part, and then gives as a general rule the
positive formula of the series.

By this logical process Proudhon so transforms property that it becomes a real, positive,

and social idea, a property which abolishes former property, and is beneficial to all.   The
whole problem is thus critically treated by him
without any sentimentality; he reduces all
Socialism to a calculation, and by this formal
act, which we will more specially consider, arrives
at the transformation of society.   Capital, says
Proudhon, has subdued property, and labour
must subdue capital.

This battle with capital pervades all the
writings of Proudhon.   He encompasses it, he
undermines it, he strangles it with its own
hands.   He is the deadly foe of capital, because
property is never more hurtful to labour than
when it appears in the form of capital.   Capital
has of itself a creative power; it works quite
independently of the capitalist while he sleeps.
It is influential even when inactive; ay, its
influence even continues when it is hidden away
and buried.

Capital is labour grown into a parvenu; and as
an upstart is hardest upon his former companions,
so capital, which represents concentrated labour,
is most severe upon labour.   It not only de-
vours the fruit of labour, but it anticipates it,
and in every phase it hangs on it like a consum-
ing sickness.

Capital is of a cannibal nature.   The capitalist
may be the noblest philanthropist, but under

the present economic arrangements of society
he has no free-will in reference to his capital.
The action of capital upon labour resembles that
of the butcher who fattens the lamb he destines
for slaughter. The support capital bestows upon
labour is the more pernicious, inasmuch as apparently it is beneficial. On the one hand, the
influence of capital upon labour is as creative and
invigorating as light upon plants. Everything
that is great and beautiful in labour emanates
from capital. Yet, on the other hand, it acts as
fire upon wood.

Socialism is not hostile to capital—in it it
sees the blessing of labour; but it fights against
interest on capital, which robs labour of all the
salutary effects it derives from it. The productivity of capital is to annihilate. The rebellion
of Socialism against capital consists only in this
tendency, and this was strongly prominent in
Proudhon.

To abolish interest on capital, to place the
workman in such a position that he may always
be able unhindered to find the means of production, to make work dependent only on itself, to
establish facility of interchange of products, and
gratuitous and mutual credit, were the Socialist
ideas which led Proudhon to a " People's Bank."
The " People's Bank," had it been realised, would
have been the retort for the distillation of society.

It was not to be a means of organisation, but
of destruction. While other Socialists sought
in vain to organise labour, Proudhon in the
" Banque du Peuple " found the means to free
it from its chains.

Proudhon is free. In the development and
comprehension of his liberty consists the pre-
sentation and conception of his revolutionary
character. He is a free man, and possesses all
the sublimity, grandeur, pride, and egotism
which accompany independence and solitude.
Never did he ally himself to a party ; he knew
no other guide but the internal instinct he possessed to further his own development. For
him there were no other laws but those of his
own nature. His love of liberty was so bound-
less that it verged on obstinacy. It irked him
to have a companion, since a companion might
acquire an influence over him. So often, therefore, as any one pursued the same path as he, he
tore himself roughly away, and preferred to seek
his goal by a circuitous route. Even the pro-
paganda of his ideas received thus a peculiar
character.

" I will neither be ruled nor rule," he once
said. This egotism went so far that he did not
even trouble himself about his disciples or his
public. All his works are monologues. This
even had great influence on his political writings.

At the moment of the scientific contest he felt himself, as it were, fastened to his antagonist, and this made his refutations so hasty, so coarse, even at times so venomous. He ended every controversy by tearing himself away from his antagonist. Only when he had broken off the controversy, and once more stood solitary, did he feel his pulse throb freely, powerfully, and full of life. His feelings then were as one who had loosed himself from a corpse to which he had been chained.

Most remarkable in this respect was his controversial interchange of letters with the only economist who waged an honourable war with him—Bastiat. We see in their correspondence how wearisome was the vicinity of Bastiat to Proudhon. Every letter is concluded with an expressed hope that it may be the last, and the following one is visibly commenced with an effort. Suddenly he tears himself away from Bastiat, and all at once concludes the contest; and his last words are, " M. Bastiat, you are a dead man !"

Proudhon was so impetuous a defender of liberty, that he was horrified at everything which restrains the liberty of the individual, even for his own benefit. He would have no mechanical, but an organic bond of society. He would have man amid the turmoil of life preserve his solitariness, the source of all great things ; and

he knew no more beautiful picture than the skiff
which, guided by a single man, is tossed about
upon the seething ocean.

Even labour was with him synonymous with
individual liberty. "When you speak of organised labour," he said in one of his pamphlets,
" it is exactly as if you undertook to gouge out
the eyes of liberty." He would have had liberty
for himself, for his antagonists, for the world.
He fought the battle with bitterness, but he
turned away shudderingly from the weapon of
reaction. Had in his time the Jesuits and Ul-
tramontanes fallen, he would have initiated no
reaction against them. Refutation alone, not
suppression, appeared to him human; and he
alone was in his view revolutionary who held
unbounded liberty as the principle of revolution.

Thus it was that he showed himself most
sublime when the Procureur-General proposed
his arrest on account of an article he had written. A motion for permission to prosecute him
was brought in to the National Assembly (February 14, 1849), and he then spoke, concluding
with these words, " Citizens! I await the decision of the Assembly without the least dis-
quietude, since I am one of those who may be
refuted but not punished!"

Everything that Proudhon proposed in reference to the mutual relations of mankind emanated

from this ardent adoration of liberty. He would
have had each man do as much service for his
fellow-man as his fellow-man did for him—not
more—not less. It is from this love of liberty
that his writings were pervaded by such a hatred
of privileges. His thirst for liberty caused him
to rebel against all and everything, even against
himself. It is on this account that his "Confessions of a Revolutionist" is one of the most remarkable books we possess. Never were such brave
words spoken by a prisoner. We stand before the
bars of his cell and listen to his words, and we
envy him his liberty. He is in the power of the
Government, and calmly proves that it has poi-
son in its veins and must fall. In his narrow cell
he annihilates the idea of government and the
rent of capital—all the bases of ancient society.
He crumbles up the world to nothing, stands
triumphantly on the universal ruin, breaks out
into an ironical song of praise, and mocks at
himself and everything else.

After he has thus, as it were, subterraneously
undermined and blown everything into the air,
suddenly he comes forth into the clear cheerful
daylight of irony; but the irony never spares its
own work, and mocks at all existing things.

Having annihilated governmentalism and
capital, he praises irony as the only true liberty.
In his solitude he concludes with sublime

laughter which is understood by few. His book
closes with these words: "Irony, true liberty! you
have saved me from the ambition of power, the
slavery of party, the admiration of great lords,
the mystification of politics, the fanaticism of
reformers, the superstition of this world, and,
chief of all, from self-deification. Thou art the
teacher of wisdom, the genius of Providence and
virtue. Goddess! that thou art! oh, come and
pour out over my fellow-citizens only one ray of
light! Send forth into their souls only the spark
of your spirit, so that my confession may conci-
liate them, and they may realise the unavoidable
revolution with joy and rejoicing."

This right of the individual to be allowed to
be free and alone Proudhon demands not only
for himself, but for every one else; and he held
those social arrangements only to be good and
reasonable in which individualism finds its fullest
development. Under present circumstances this
is not the case, because the individual is governed;
his activity is restricted. Proudhon therefore
regarded that condition as an ideal one in which
government and society should be identical and
no longer divided.

This return of government to its original
source, this reflux of labour into national life, is
for him the type of freedom. His view of the
present State was mankind despairing at his-

tory, it was the violent rending asunder of the chains which for a thousand years have fettered liberty. It is the confession that it is contradictory to the dignity of humanity to be ruled, that a transference of authority, whether to a monarch or to a popular representative, is a lie and a cheat.

His anarchy does not dissolve : it creates. It is the purest human form, the necessity of freedom ; it gives an impulse to self-assertion and independence ; by it the masses arrive at their majority, and feel at first uneasy at the new sense of responsibility thereby imparted.

The abolition of the present State is the creation of the true state, of the first free human system of solidarity in which every individual rises to his true value, and human affairs be carried on in a purer and more vigorous fashion than heretofore. His abolition of government is the introduction of self-government, the organisation of universal suffrage, the absorption of all activities for the free development of the most glorious goal of humanity.

Proudhon regards the regulation of the free attitude of individual to individual as the only problem of social science. He saw the whole evil of our present social condition in the fact that it misunderstood and violated reciprocity. Hence it was that, economically, his whole endeavours were directed to the establishment of justice in exchange, to the organisation of credit, of true mutuality. As he began by freeing the individual from the ties of State and of humanity, and by setting him up in his full right as an individual, so he led back all free individuals to the true human fraternity.

This union, springing from a purified egotism, was not comprised in the Communist solidarity of Louis Blanc, but in a mutual solidarity.

On the one side, Proudhon descried the independent centralisation of the social functions; on the other, the mutual guaranteeing of credit. His entire scheme for society was exhausted in these two formulas. He led us by egotism to true fraternity, or, in other words, he overcame egotism by itself. The economic side of his principle gains by this means, as we shall see, a profound meaning. He tears from the hand of capital its own weapon wherewith to kill it.

The business of exchange he transforms into a revolution, and he uses the means formerly at the disposal of usury wherewith to liberate labour. Capitalists obtained possession of the bill of exchange, and made of it a monopoly. Proudhon restores this invention to society at large. He generalises and democratises the bill of exchange, he republicanises credit, and thereby creates a true solidarity which forms the exact antithesis of Communism.

CHAPTER VI.

HUMANITY, since the turning-point of modern history, is going through a course of symbol renunciation, in order to turn towards the reality of thought.

In Egypt it was hieroglyphics, in Greece sculpture, in the Middle Ages architecture, which served as an allegory. The mystical twilight of history has now been changed. Government and the Church are the last symbols which man has not yet got rid of. Authority and religion represent the range of the ideas of humanity, because it cannot yet breathe the purity of the idea.

Government and God are intimately connected. There is a meaning in the expression used by kings, " By the grace of God." Without God there is no king, without a king there is no God. Man decks these last remnants of his mystical immaturity with all imaginable colours.

Man invented statecraft, by which the symbol of government can be transformed into an intellectual reality; and he illuminates the hieroglyphic of religion by the eternal flame of philosophy, without knowing that thereby it must be destroyed.

Hieroglyphics must be believed in, or they cease to exist. Man, however, endeavours to explain to himself the governmental and religious symbolism, in order to preserve it by reason, and thus unintentionally solves the problem of the century—namely, the desertion of symbolism and the adoption of reality.

He only is a Christian who believes in the redemption of the world by the death of Jesus Christ, and he only is a true citizen of the State to whom the king patriarchally represents and symbolises the entire State.

As soon as criticism of the mystical contents of religion commences, or as soon as we cease to recognise in the king the genuine symbolic expression of the whole body of citizens, to supplement his powers with national representatives, and to demand guarantees, the transition path to ideal purity has been entered upon, which man strives, both as a philosopher and a citizen, to attain.

Hitherto most men have been only able to fathom their position in the universe by means of a God external to the world and earthly culture. The necessity for a social organisation of union only presents itself figuratively to human consciousness by the establishment of a government. The more clear is the self-assertion of the individual, the stronger is the impulse to achieve and satisfy it, and therefore the less is it contented with symbols. A thing becomes a symbol sooner than a man. There are, therefore, no more governments, only usurpations. Opposition to the State is one of the chief features of our age; it alone gives sense and meaning to revolution.

Practically, a revolution is only thereby important that it denotes the struggle of nations to get rid of the morbid matter of government—the State. During the victory of a revolution the people is for one moment free, and lives long on the memory of this moment.

But immediately after the victory mistrust and discontent slink in among the people. Without knowing why, each one feels that this wild fanatical state of affairs, this morbidly heightened wantonness, this mutual animosity, as little constitutes freedom as the recommencement of governing, decreeing, place-hunting, and organising can achieve any real alteration. Discontented and deceived, we are deafened in the wild tumult of the revolution. Happily the unhealthy wave of life which is thrown up does not leave us time to consider whether the battle has been really useful, and whether the victims

G

which have been slain have been offered in a noble cause.

But when sobriety sets in, the old chains are once more felt, the old complaints of having been cheated are once more raised, and the firm resolve is taken, having learned something by experience, to do it better next time. As if the chain had not again been rattled the very day after the revolution, only we did not hear the clank. As if the political strife had not been waged the very day after the fall of the Government; and as if by the juggle of election, we had not been worse defrauded of our liberty by the democrats than a countryman of his money by a common thimble-rigger. Let the revolution but take a name, let it be personified, whether in Robespierre or Lamartine, and it shrivels up and is lost.

Philanthropists and politicians are the bane of revolutions: the former, because they will not leave the people to themselves, but will always be doing something for them; the latter, because they create parties, and thereby the ambitious struggle for power. The greatest revolution will therefore be achieved when we revolt no more, but only resolve. The true will of the people is greater than any revolution. All revolutionary movements only overthrow one government to set up another; but we do not dispute the sublimity of the error which is involved in a revolution.

Every rebel is a genius; to rebel is to be in
advance of the age, to make a leap out of the
State, to fly against the Government. A revolution is a species of birth, a coming of age, a
mystical idea of liberty. Every barricade is an
altar of liberty, a negation of police regulations,
a humorous criticism of the State, a stumbling-
block which trips up the State.

Still revolution never reaches its goal, because
it is always cheated; and so fast as it cuts off
one head from the Hydra government, another
starts up. For instance, France succeeded in
escaping from Louis XVI. to fall into the hands
of Robespierre; then came the France of Napoleon,
Louis XVIII., Charles X., Louis Philippe, Lamartine, Cavaignac, Louis Napoleon, and Thiers.
But the France which belongs to no one, and
therefore to every Frenchman, is still to come.

Government is the tool, to obtain which avarice
and ambition strive; it is the sword with which
now this, now that one strikes and hits, and
calls it governing. We shall constantly be
struck and wounded, let who will wield the sword,
until we have destroyed the weapon itself.

Hitherto the sovereignty of the people has
alone been sought after, but we must achieve
the sovereignty of each separate individual. The
sovereignty of the people is an abstract empty
idea, good for nothing but the fiction of trans-

ferring the sovereignty of the people to a king. The uniform is the true symbol of the State. The fewer gaps exist in the constitution of the State, the more zealously is the uniformity of individuals carried out. Despotism does not allow the single individual to count; Constitutionalism gives him only a little paint; the Republic plays with its booty: in every form of government we are the victims of the State. By it we are crippled, with our mother's milk we imbibe the submission which makes us serviceable to the State. Only a few thinkers have hitherto escaped the State, and while in horror they have been gazing back at the monster, in order to divulge the enigma, they have been swallowed up by it.

A bloody line goes through the history of every people and of all times. It divides mankind into hostile camps, and on both sides blind hatred and a spirit of persecution are ranged. This line it is which divides parties; where they come in contact, there do prejudice, hatred, persecution, and murder break out.

Faction has already demanded millions of corpses, rivers of blood, and the older mankind becomes, the wider is the gulf. We stagger on the brink, an overpowering giddiness seizes us, and we are precipitated into it.

What is the meaning of all these victims of party? what significance is there in these countless corpses? what do we read in their stark pale features? Why cannot the sublime peace of the humanitarian idea calm this barbarous fever glow? Why do we go so far as to estimate the culture of a nation by the perfection of its factions? What unholy fire is it that burns within us, and causes us to shrink back from the sobriety and self-advantageousness of absence of party? Why is it that we nevertheless comprehend how the artist who lives in a world of beauty need belong to no party in order to fulfil his high human calling?

Is party strife in accordance with the laws of life and history? Can only hatred and murder maintain the world? must the earth drink blood in order to go on? Is life synonymous with strife? the return of harmony and of love synonymous with nothingness and destruction? Has nature imparted to us the charm of colour, only that thereby the standards of party may be designated? Is there no salvation from faction? can we not in love fulfil the law of history —namely, Progress by Antithesis.

Is faction a necessity? and is it only by chance that it becomes a reality through birth and station, speech and nationality, labour and capital? Cannot the present mediate peaceably between the past and the future? or must the past be murdered, and the future receive a baptism of blood?

Is there no peaceful solution for the combatants of humanity? Dreadful thought! And yet even party faction is a witness against the State. Faction is abhorrence at government. We struggle to be ruled in a certain manner, yet we fall into the error of desiring to govern in our own way. Every party is only so near the truth as it prevents another coming into power and ruling. All parties must devour each other until not one remains. The quarrels of parties among themselves serve progress and truth. The development of humanity will never assume any other form than that induced by faction. But the noxious, confining influence of faction can be destroyed. The horror and the bloodshed of party strife will cease, and only the blessing which arises out of their contradictory natures will remain, when government no more exists, or, what is the same, when there is no party desiring to rule another.

Every man lives in his fellow-man, and is forced by a mighty impulse to care for him. From this mighty impulse to benefit his neighbour springs all faction. Therefore humanity cannot be lost, it cannot fall to pieces and dissolve. This impulse binds men faster together than the State. The hatred engendered by civil war has its roots only in the State, and all love is sucked out by government.

CHAPTER VII.

IN this sense Proudhon was the greatest rebel.
He accused all our State dispositions of being
impregnated with feudality and monarchy. Our
system of administration, in its pyramidal form,
was in his eyes essentially monarchical. The
whole power of the nation appears to him to be
concentrated in a national assembly as in a
dynasty. To him the electoral forms of the
Assembly are a mystery and a game of chance.
Proudhon does not abolish the State by an
abstract development, but he undermines it by
placing by its side the picture of no-State, a condition without government. He makes us free by
showing us liberty. Practically, this way is the
best. Man holds it impossible to escape from
his state ; a step out of his circle is for him a
journey into the unknown. Proudhon invents,
therefore, if we may use the expression, an em-
pirical way. The State belongs to empiricism,
he therefore regards its abolition as a matter of
experience.

Such an impulse to shake off the State gets

possession of his soul that he scarcely leaves himself time to find abstract grounds for it, but brings before us single examples of no-State as a reality.

This negation of the State, which not only destroys but also at the same time creates, is the only rational one. By every other means we run our heads against a prison wall, and believe we are thereby achieving our liberty. While to most men the abolition of the State is synonymous with nothingness, Proudhon sees so clearly the bright picture of a society without any form of State, that he complains of not being a painter or a mechanician, in order to be able to represent it in its entirety.

With him anarchy is not blank despair in the State, nor does it possess a sweet mystical charm to hurl itself into an unknown void; whereas many men who preach after him do not grasp this deep sense, and are only charmed at having discovered a vocal expression for their dull impulse towards suicide, and to be able to translate their pollution and dissolution into the ideal.

The doctrine of the abolition of the State has a something terrible, synonymous with madness, for sober practical men who love laws and order; but for those who have lost themselves, who live without object or aim, and hate forms, it has a charm. While the one set of men see in the no-

State theory the impossibility of realising their active healthy impulse for achievements, to the others the general dissolution and decay are especially welcome. They feel their own death-agony, and rejoice to carry with them this world full of pulsating glorious power. This struggle seems to them only the natural vocation of life and the world; in their slothful egotistical nothingness, they cheer on the new prophet of anarchy and the abolition of the State, just as once ignorant weak minds accepted the doctrine of community of goods and wives.

But Proudhon is as little understood by these friends as by his other enemies. In this branch of his criticism he still remains the cold impassive book-keeper; he calculates the State to its death, even as he throttled capital with figures. He addresses those of his readers whom he regards as unbelievers, before he proceeds to demonstrate the possibility of abolishing the State, thus: "My development can only let matters follow one upon another, and not present everything at once. How, therefore, shall we be able to grasp the entirety? What guarantee shall we have for our constitution? This guarantee. I will name it. It is so simple that every one can prove its accuracy. It consists of a mathematical expression. 'All the parts together equal the whole.' Reader, do you

believe in mathematics? If so, you can entrust
yourself entirely to my guidance. I will show
you the most interesting things, and you run no
danger of losing yourselves. By aid of this expression I hope to show you the real unheard-of
play, that government by the progress of social
reforms necessarily falls, and in proportion as it
falls must order take its place."

Thus, as he raises his axe to shatter the State,
he calls out to his readers to help him count the
broken fragments, and from their number to
conclude that the whole still exists in the total
amount of the pieces. It is as if during dooms-
day he geometrically calculated the downfall of
the world.

This cold, sober habit of destruction, passion-
less as that of an executioner, enabled him to
reason out the extinction of the State; and we
are thereby pacified that in the loss of the State
nothing will be really lost, because this eternal
calculator certainly took everything into account.

Proudhon was so sure that he asked, "What
shall we do the day after the Revolution?" He
was so certain that he mocks and gibes at the
Socialist writers with their quacksalver remedies,
and at the Mountain, with its idea gathered from
the National Convention, that "the people are
the starting-point of all government, that for
the last time they have to carry on the Govern-

ment in order to end the Revolution in twenty-
four hours by decrees."

He would have strangled the State with its
own hands, with laws, and have commenced the
kingdom of anarchy with well-considered decrees.
His departure out of the State was therefore no
act of fever or precipitation, of satiety and
eccentricity, of aimlessness, of want of a definite
idea, but it is the sober result of the conviction
that we had not yet ended the Revolution, that
every revolution must negate and clear away
something, and that two things especially were
to be denied and cleared away—the exhaustion
of humanity by capital, and oppression by the
State; on this double negation depended the
regeneration of society.

We are so accustomed to Governments and
States, that we regard human society as a State,
and consider the negation of the State as synonymous with utter dismemberment and isolation.
Many persons might therefore define Proudhon's
idea of the abolition of the State, that every one
should be for himself and by himself, and no
one should trouble himself about his neighbour.
Yet man is only free by means of his neighbour;
he lives only by means of his neighbour; he is
only happy by means of his neighbour. This is
the mystical human view of existence. It was
this mighty impulse which animated Leonidas

at Thermopylæ, and which drove the Parisians to storm the Bastille.

Rightly, then, did Proudhon discriminate between simple and compound liberty. The first only exists among barbarians, and even only among civilised nations, so long as they alone feel free when isolated. In this way he is the freest whose activity is least restrained by other men. A single man alone upon the wide earth would represent the highest grade of this liberty.

Against this sterile liberty, brooking no witnesses, Proudhon took up the social standpoint, and in it found liberty and solidarity so synonymous that the liberty of one man is not bounded by the liberty of another man, as was expressed in the Declaration of Rights in 1793, but rather finds therein an ally, and he is the freest man who is most closely connected with his equals.

He exemplifies this by two nations separated from each other by an arm of the sea or a chain of mountains. These nations are comparatively free so long as they have no intercourse with each other; but they are poor—they are simply free. But they are far freer and richer if they interchange their products. This he called compound liberty. The special activity of these two nations acquired greater scope when they mutually exchange articles of consumption and labour.

" This simple fact," says Proudhon, " reveals to
us an entire system of new developments of
liberty, a system in which the exchange of produce is but the first step." With these words
he alluded to his " People's Bank."

Proudhon, therefore, did not despair of civilisation. He did not regard it as the misfortune of
mankind, and would not allow the citizens to
slink back to the woods. The abolition of the
State did not appear to him as a hostile isolation
of mankind. What he wanted was the State
without government, without tutelage ; the perfect free right of each single individual who in
his fellows finds his completeness and progress,
the self-administration and self-government of
all members of society. He did not want that
every mouthful we eat should be first chewed by
the teeth of an official. All the countless supports which the State has erected to save us
from falling, but which finally form prison bars,
he would have cleared away—the cessation of all
protection by the State, which makes us cowardly
and drowsy—and in their places self-protection ;
then would liberty, equality, and fraternity become a reality.

In every society Proudhon distinguished two
kinds of constitution—the social and the political. The abolition of the latter was with him
synonymous with abolition of the State. As

an example of a social constitution, Proudhon
brought forward the Ten Commandments which
Moses gave to the Jews. Those, and the accom-
panying laws which regulate religious ceremonies
and lay down police and sanitary regulations,
form no political constitution. The theocratic
form of government which the national bond
assumed, but which under Samuel led to the
establishment of a kingdom, did not at first at
all take the character of a political organisation
because religion and society were synonymous.

The essential sign of a political constitution
consists in the division of the powers—that is, the
discrimination of two phases in the government,
a legislative and an executive ; and this discrimination results in government, which ought to be
the instrument of the people becoming its
master.

Proudhon historically deduced from the example of the last French republican constitution the origin of this division of powers.
" Why do we want a constitution ? " said some
respected members of the Constituent Assembly.
" What use is this division of power, with all the
ambition and danger which follow in its train ?
Is it not enough that an assembly which is the
expression of the will of the people should make
laws, and have them executed by its own ministers ? " Thereupon the friends of the constitu-

tional system replied, after Rousseau: "The division of powers has its ground in centralisation itself. It is unavoidable in a State composed of several millions of men who are unable themselves daily to take part in public affairs. It is also a guarantee of liberty, since the rule of an assembly is as terrible as that of a prince, and, besides, it lacks responsibility. Yes! The despotism of an assembly is one hundred times worse than the autocracy of a single man.

Proudhon considered these objections so important that he regarded the government by a convention as the worst kind of government. He sought the solution of the political problem by harmonising liberty with centralisation. The separation of the powers of the State, which it was desired to introduce as an attempt to secure liberty, proved insufficient. Still the despotism of legislative assemblies arises without separating the State powers. But let every centre be done away with, let centralisation of every kind be given up, and still we should drift into meaningless Federalism; the State would crumble into nothingness, and the Republic lose its unity.

What, therefore, must be striven for is the reconciliation of liberty with centralisation. As Proudhon sets himself this task, he diverges from that anarchical party which would set up

in place of the State mere single unconnected
communities, or even mere individuals, and
which sees in the common prosecution of any
object a return to the system of State.

He pointed out, as the result of the Republic
of 1848, that no constitution can keep its pro-
mises; that it is utilised, according to the pleasure of the governments, at one time for the
furtherance of reaction, at another of progress;
that the one-half of its clauses contradict the
other half; and that inevitably it must establish a false and corrupt basis of society.

CHAPTER VIII.

LONG before Proudhon, Jeremy Bentham, Elias Regnault, and others, revealed the whole sophistry of parliamentary institutions, but they did not go beyond empty complaint and fruitless denial.

Proudhon allowed mankind first, as it were, to despair in order to save it. He derided the work of the Constitution—the emanation of three revolutions—and showed that the blood-bedabbled daughter of revolution was but a lifeless woodblock. He looked at the corpses of the revolutionary combatants, and he laughed; he scoffed at their achievements; every single gem of the Constitution which we rejoice at, he tore out, broke up, and then showed us that it was but paste.

Socialists complained that the right to work has not been admitted in the Constitution. Proudhon rejoiced that his utterance against theirs, "Give me the right to labour, and I will leave you the right to property," had hindered, as is supposed, this admission. He could, he observed, have explained that his words intended no threat

H

against property, but he did not in order that his country might be spared this new constitutional lie.

In place of this right to labour, the authors of the Constitution inserted the right to public assistance in their document,—as Proudhon remarks, " Nonsense in place of an impossibility." He drove the Constitution out of its last ambush, and cried out bitterly: " As if I could not have said, Give me the right to assistance, and I will leave you the right to labour."

And then he calmly declared what the right to public assistance was. He showed that what was placed before us as an alms, was as such impossible; but elevated to a right, it opened a gulf and led straight to civil war. With the malicious joy of a cheat, who having effected his swindle, reveals to his victim his *modus operandi*, he demonstrated that against the same subterfuge, which might again be used as a guarantee against the right to public assistance, the same objection might be repeated again and again.

According to him, all the political and economic elements on which society rests mutually make each other complete, pass one into the other, and by turns consume each other. Society rests entirely on these contrasts and assimilations which all return to each other, and the system is eternal. And the solution of the social problem consists in not allowing the various expressions to come forward as contrasts, as was the case in the first formation of society, but to treat them as deductions : thus, for instance, that the rights to labour, to credit, to public assistance—the realisation of which was under an antagonistic legislation impossible or dangerous—following one upon the other from an already existing and undoubted right, should mutually guarantee each other, we admit, as emanating from the right of free competition. It is only our utter ignorance of these transformations which makes us blind to our own resources, and causes us always to lay down a guarantee in the text of our constitutions which no power of the Government can give us, but which we can achieve for ourselves.

Thus it is that Proudhon describes every right which is based upon a Government as an empty relief. Of universal suffrage he remarks :— " How can it be true when it is only used in ambiguous questions ? How can it express the true opinion of the people when this people by inequality of means is divided into two classes, which, when they vote, are either governed by servility or hatred ? Can the same people, held in check, by the powers of Government, give any opinion upon anything ? Is the exercise of its rights confined to electing its leaders and char-

latans every three or four years? Does its
reason, resting upon the antagonism of interests
and ideas only, move from one contrast to
another? And can it in consequence of the
existence of party hatred, only escape one danger by plunging into another? Society under
the 200 francs franchise was immovable, but
since the introduction of universal suffrage it
constantly revolves on the same axis. Formerly
it stagnated in its lethargy; now it is giddy.
Have we therefore advanced? Are we richer or
freer because we have created a million of little
revolving wheels?"

Thus Proudhon demonstrates that the Constitution of 1848 could give no guarantees either for
labour, credit, public assistance, education, progress, universal suffrage, or anything else which
might tend to advance either social or political
well-being. On this point he continues thus:—
" In my opinion, the fault of every constitution,
be it social or political, which brings on conflicts
and generates antagonism in society, consists on
the one side (taking for an example the present
French Constitution) in the badly completed and
imperfect separation of powers, or to speak more
correctly, of functions: on the other side, in the
insufficiency of centralisation.

" Thence it follows that the collective power
remains without activity, and the collective idea,

or universal suffrage, without reality. We must
end this scarcely commenced separation and
centralise still more. We must give back to
universal suffrage its rights, that is, to the
people the energy and activity which they lack.

"This is the principle: to prove this, to explain the social mechanism, I can now suitably
dispense with deductions. Examples are sufficient. Here, as in all exact sciences, the practice
is the theory; the precise observation of fact is
the science itself.

"For many centuries the spiritual has been
separated from the secular power in accordance
with the adduced formula. By the way, I may
remark, that the political principle of separation
of powers or functions is one and the same as
the economic principle of the separation of
industries and the division of labour. On this
point we see the identity of the political and
social constitution already foreshadowed. Now,
I hold that the spiritual and secular powers have
never been wholly separated, that consequently,
their centralisation, to the great detriment of
the Church Government and of believers, has
always been unsatisfactory. The separation
would be complete if the secular power ceased to
mix itself up in the celebration of the mysteries,
the administration of the sacrament, in the management of the parishes, and also took no part

in the appointment of bishops. Centralisation
would be greater, and the Government far more
regular, if the people in every parish had the
right not only to elect their pastor, vicar, or, if
they pleased, none at all, if the priests of every
diocese elected their bishops, if the Assembly of
Bishops alone had the power of regulating religious affairs, theological education, and public
worship. By this means the clergy would cease
to be an instrument of tyranny over the
people in the hands of the political Government.
By this application of universal suffrage the
clerical regiment, which is centralised in itself,
receiving its inspirations from the people, and
not from the Government or the Pope, would
remain in constant harmony with the requirements of society, and with the moral and intellectual condition of the citizens.

   " But what do we see in place of this democratic and rational system?   Certainly the
Government has nothing to do with questions
of public worship; it does not teach the Cate-
chism, or give instruction in the seminaries.
But it selects the bishops, and the bishops select
the priests and vicars, and send them, without
in the least consulting the people, into the
parishes; so that Church and State, intimately
connected one with the other, though often
quarrelling, form a species of offensive and

defensive alliance against the liberty and autonomy of the people. This joint Government,
instead of serving the country, oppresses it. It
would be useless to enumerate the various results
of such a state of affairs; they are palpable to
every one.

"Therefore to regain organic, economic, and
social truth, the constitutional *cumulus* must first
be abolished, by depriving the State of the right
to appoint bishops, and sharply dividing spiritual
from secular affairs; secondly, the Church must
be centralised in itself by a system of graduated
elections; thirdly, the clerical power, like every
other in the State, must be based upon universal
suffrage. This system transforms the present
Government into a simple administration; all
France, so far as regards clerical functions, will
be centralised.

"By this simple fact of the electoral initiative
the people thus governs in sacred as in secular
matters, is itself governed no more. And we can
easily imagine that if it were possible to introduce an organisation of secular affairs throughout
the whole country, with similar bases to that
proposed, for the administration of clerical
affairs, the most perfect tranquillity and the most
powerful centralisation would obtain, without the
existence of anything of what we of the present
day call established authority or government.

" One more instance. Formerly, in addition
to the legislative and executive, a third power
was reckoned, the judicial. It was a deviation
from the separating dualism, a first step towards
the complete separation of the political functions
as of the industrial forces. The constitution of
1848, after the pattern of those of 1814 and
1830, speaks of only one judicial class.

" Class, power, or function I find here, as in
the Church, a fresh example of cumulus by the
State, and therefore a fresh wrong done to the
sovereignty of the people.

" The various specialities of the judicial functions, their hierarchy, the irremovability of the
judges, their cohesion under a single monarchy,
all show a tendency towards centralisation. But
the judges do not in the least stand under the rule
of those persons for whose benefit they were appointed ; they are entirely at the disposal of the
executive power, and are not by election subordinate to the country, to the president, or prince
by appointment.

" Thus it happens that those persons for whose
benefit judges are appointed are just as much
handed over to their own natural judges as the
parishioners to their priest; and the people
become the heritage of the officials ; the plaintiff
is for the judge, not the judge for the plaintiff.

" But let universal suffrage and a graduated

system of election be adopted for the judicial as
for the clerical function; let the irremovability
of judges, that surrender of the right of election,
be abolished; let the State be deprived of all
power and influence over the judicial body; and
let this exclusively centralised class stand only
under the people, and the most powerful instrument of tyranny would have been taken from
the governing power. The administration of
justice will then become a principle of liberty
and order. And if we do not assume that the
people from whom, by means of universal suffrage, all power emanates, is in contradiction
with itself, that it requires in the administration
of justice a different system to what it requires
in religious matters and *vice versâ*, we can rely
upon it that this division of power will bring
about no conflict. We can calmly lay down the
fundamental law that separation and equilibrium
are synonymous.

"I come now to another sequence of ideas:
the military system. Is it not true that the
army belongs to the Government? That it, by
permission of the constitutional dreamers, belongs far less to the country than to the State?
Formerly the general staff of the army was the
military court. Under the Empire, the united
corps d'élite were called the Old and Young
Imperial Guard. Every year the Government

takes, but the country does not give, 80,000 conscripts.   Government in the interest of its policy, and to carry out its will, appoints commanders, orders the movements of the troops, at the same time as it disarms the National Guards. The despotism of its armed force, of its noblest blood, does not appertain to the nation which arms for liberty and glory.   Thus here again social order is endangered, not from want of centralisation, but in consequence of defective division.

"The people has a confused idea of this preposterous condition of affairs, since in every revolution the withdrawal of the troops is urgently insisted upon.   Also a law on the recruitment and organisation of the National Guards and the army is demanded.   And the authors of the Constitution marked well this danger when, in Art. 50, they ordained that the President of the Republic has at his disposal the armed force, without, however, commanding it in person.   Really !   Wise lawgivers !   And what object is obtained in his not commanding it in person, if he appoints the commanders, if, according to his good pleasure, he can send them to Rome or Mogador, if he can dispense advancement, orders, and pensions, if he has generals who command in his stead ?

"It belongs to the citizens hierarchically to

appoint their military commanders, since the
soldiers and National Guards would choose the
persons to fill the lower and the officers the
upper grades.   Thus organised the army retains
its feeling of citizenship, and is no longer a
nation in a nation, a fatherland in a fatherland;
no longer a wandering colony where the citizen,
naturalised as a soldier, learns to fight against
his own country.   It is the nation itself centralised in its strength and youth, independent
of the Government, which cannot command it
or dispose of it as now, when every judicial
functionary or police agent can, in the name of
the law, invoke the armed power.   In times of
war, the army only owes obedience to the National Assembly and the commanders appointed
by it.

" When the humanitarians among the Socialists see these papers, they will perhaps ask if I
look upon public worship, justice, and war as
eternal institutions, and if it is really worth the
while of a reformer to take so much trouble for
their organisation ?   But it is clear that all this
does not in the least prejudice the necessity and
essence of these great utterances of the social
thought, and that we if we would appeal to the
sole competent verdict of the people as to the independence and duration of these institutions, have
nothing else to do but to give them, as I have

already said, a democratic institution. Religion
and justice belong to that class of things which
I have called organic, and it is for the people
alone to decide whether it is to be overthrown
or maintained. Every other initiative in this
direction would be either tyranny or deception.
In war at least every one recognises a sad necessity which will doubtless be abolished by the
progress of liberty. Will you anticipate this
abolition by some centuries? Then begin by
separating and centralising the functions, by
disarming government. I now proceed.

"In all times society felt the necessity of
protecting its trade and industry against foreign
importation. The power or function which pro-
tects home labour and secures for it its natural
market is the customs authority. On this point
I will in no wise give an opinion as to the
morality or immorality, the use or otherwise, of
the customs system. I take it as society gives
it to me, and confine myself to investigating it
from the stand-point of the constitution of
powers. Later on, when we come from the
political and social to the purely economic question, we shall attempt to arrive at a proper
solution; we shall see if home produce can be
protected without dues and supervision : in one
word, if we can do without the customs authority.

"By the simple fact of its existence, the cus-

toms authority is a neutralised function; its
origin, as its sphere of operation, excludes every
idea of dismemberment. How comes it, then,
that this function, which officially belongs to
merchants and traders, which could exclusively
be managed by chambers of commerce, is also
dependent on the State? France supports an
army of more than 40,000 men for the protection of its trade, toll-collectors all armed with
sword and gun, and who also annually cost the
country twenty-six millions. The object which
this army has constantly in view is simultane-
ously to wage war upon smugglers, and to
collect a duty upon imported and exported goods
of from 100 to 110 millions.

"But who can know better than the trade
itself where and how much it requires protection,
what productions require premiums? And as
regards the customs service, are not the parties
interested palpably justified in calculating the
expense, and not the Government, in making
out of it a source of emolument for its creatures,
and in seeking in the differential duties levied a
means to carry on its extravagance? As long
as the customs administration remains in the
hands of the authorities, so long will the pro-
tective system, on which subject as a system I
pass no opinion, necessarily be defective. It
will lack honesty and fairness. The tariffs im-

posed by the customs authorities are an exaction,
and smuggling, in the words of the Honourable
M. Blanqui, is a right and a duty.

" Besides the ministers of public worship,
justice, war, of international trade or customs,
Government cumulates other functions—namely,
of agriculture and commerce, of public education, and finally, to pay all these officials, the
ministry of finance. Our alleged division of
power is only a cumulation of all powers; our
centralisation only a sham.

" Does it not appear to you that the farmers,
who are already organised by their common aim,
could effect their centralisation, and thoroughly
watch over their common interests without
needing the hand of the State? That tradesmen,
manufacturers, and the industrial classes generally, who in their chambers of commerce have
an already existing groundwork, could equally
organise a central administration, even at their
own expense, without the interference of the
Government, without looking for advantages
from its arbitrary favour, or ruin from its inex-
perience, that they are not able to discuss their
affairs in general assemblies, to enter into
association with other bodies, and to pass all
requisite resolutions without the *visa* of the
President of the Republic? That they could
confer upon one of themselves the task of

carrying out their decisions, to one of their equals, to one elected by themselves, who should thus be a Minister?

"The Public Works, which concern all, whether connected with agriculture, industry, or trade, departments or parishes, might be divided among the local and central administrations interested, and no longer form monopolising official systems, as do now the army and the customs—a special corporation exclusively embodied in the State—a corporation which has everything, hereditary privilege and Ministry, in order that the State may juggle away mines, canals, and railways, may gamble in stocks and shares, grant concessions to good friends for 99 years, give away contracts for roads, bridges, harbours, dykes, excavations, sluices, dredgings, &c., to a legion of jobbers, cheats, and swindlers, who live upon the property of other people, on the hard earnings of mechanics and day-labourers, on the stupidity of the State?

"Do you not believe that public education would be as accessible and as well conducted, that the selection of the teachers, professors, rectors, and inspectors would be as happy, that the system of public instruction would be as complete if the communal and general councils were convoked to transfer education to the teachers, while the university had only to give

them their diplomas, if, as in the military system, length of service in the lower grades were
a condition of advancement, if every dignitary
of the university had first to perform the duties
of an elementary teacher?   Do you believe that
this thoroughly democratic arrangement of the
discipline of the schools would be detrimental to
the morality of education, to the dignity of
instruction, or the peace of families?   And as
the nerve of every administration is money, and
the budget is for the country, not the country
for the budget; as the taxes must every year be
voted by the popular representatives; as this is
an inalienable right of the nation under a
monarchy as under a republic; as expenditure
and revenue must both be considered by the
country before the Government can use them;
do you not see that the consequence of this
financial initiative, specially allotted to the
citizens, must be, that the ministry of finance—
in fact, the entire fiscal organisation—belongs to
the country and not to the prince?   That it
directly belongs to those who pay, and not to
those who consume the budget?   That far less
misuse and waste of the State funds would appear
if the State had as little power of disposal over
the public monies as over public worship, justice,
the army, the customs, public instruction, and
public works?

"After what I have already adduced, I will not quote more examples; the continuation of the list were easy, and the distinction between centralisation and cumulation, between separation of the legislative functions and separation of the two abstractions, which absurdly enough are called the legislative and executive powers, would be comprehended, and the difference between administration and government would be finally understood.

"Do you not believe that, with this strictly democratic system of unity, more strictness in the expenditure, punctuality of service, responsibility of officials, more courtesy, less fawning and fewer quarrels, in one word, less disorder, would prevail? Do you believe that reforms would then appear so difficult? That the influence of the authorities would falsify the decisions of the citizens, that we should not be a hundred times less governed, but our affairs a hundred times better administered?

"It was held that to re-establish national unity all the powers of the State must be placed in the hands of one single authority. But as it was soon perceived that this led up to despotism, the next idea was that a remedy could be found in a dualism of power. As if no other means existed to prevent a conflict between the Govern-

I

ment and the people than a conflict between the
Government and the Government !

" To achieve unity in a nation, centralisation
in religious, judicial, military, agricultural,
trade, commercial, and financial matters, is
requisite—in one word, in all institutions and
offices. Centralisation must ascend from the
lowest to the highest, from the outside to the
centre. All functions must be independent, and
each must govern itself.

" Place the heads of these various administrations together, and you have your council of ministers, your executive power, which can dispense
with the council of state. Place over all this a
grand jury directly appointed by the country, legis-
lature, or national assembly, empowered, not to
appoint ministers—they have been elected by the
country—but to examine accounts, pass laws,
draw up the budget, arrange differences between
the various departments—in short, to see to everything appertaining to the Ministry of the Interior,
to which the entire Government is reduced—and
you will then have a system of centralisation,
stronger, more extended, and with far more
responsibility, the more sharply the separation
of the powers is defined. You have at one and
the same time a political and a social constitution. Then would Government, State, or Power,
whatever we may call it, be reduced to an

equitable standard, with no legislative or executive functions, but be simply a spectator in the public life like the Attorney-General in legal proceedings. It would only serve to interpret the meaning of the laws, to reconcile existing contradictions, and exercise the necessary police functions.

" Thus would Government be nothing more than the mouthpiece of society, the sentinel of the people. Or rather, no government at all would exist—order would have emanated from anarchy. Then you would have liberty of the citizen, truthfulness in the institutions, purity of universal suffrage, blameless administration, impartial justice, patriotism of bayonets, overthrow of parties, the united endeavour of the universal will. Your society would be organised, live, advance, think, speak, act like one man, and the reason would be because it would no longer be represented by one man, because in it, as in every organised and living being, as in the single idea of Pascal, the centre is everywhere, the circumference nowhere."

" Our democratic traditions, our revolutionary tendencies, our need for centralisation and unity, our love of liberty and equality, and the purely economic, if badly employed principle of all our constitutions, lead us irresistibly to the anti-governmental constitution.

" I should have liked to make the Constituent Assembly understand this, had they been in a country to hear anything but commonplaces, had they not, in their blind prejudice against every new idea, in their dishonest provocations of the Socialists, always held the opinion, ' Dare to convince me ' . . . Assemblies, like nations, learn only by misfortune. We have not yet suffered enough ; we have not been sufficiently chastised for our monarchical servility and our rage for Government that we should soon love liberty and order.

" Everything with us is still a conspiracy for the object of exhausting man by man, and to govern man by man. Louis Blanc requires a strong Government to carry out what he calls good, that is his system, and to fight against evil, that is what is *not* his system. Léon Faucher requires a strong and inexorable Government to restrain the Republicans, and root out the Socialists ; all for the honour of Malthus and English political economy. M. Thiers and M. Guizot want a quasi-absolute government in order to be able to display their great talents as equilibrists.

" What sort of a nation is that from which an ordinary man must banish himself because he finds no people to govern, no parliaments to contend with, no intrigues to be woven with other governments? Messieurs Falloux and Montalembert require divine government, before which every knee shall bend, and every head bow down, and every conscience submit, in order that kings may be the gensdarmes of the popes, who are the representatives of God on earth. M. Odillon Barrot requires a double government, a legislative and an executive, in order that parliamentary opposition should always continue, and that society in this or that life should have no other object but to be the spectator of parliamentary representation."

The movement of the working classes reflected more and more the influence of Proudhon's ideas as the workmen felt the sharp points and asperities of the State.

After the June revolution a great change took place in the tendencies of the people of Paris. The influence of Louis Blanc yielded to that of Proudhon. Proudhon told the workmen neither to accept or demand anything from the State. The experience which the workmen gained in the debate on the right to labour made them regard the State as something more and more hostile to their interests. The union of all workmen's associations proved that the associations thoroughly understood that the solution of the social problem must come from below and not from above. This attempt at

union miscarried, but the influence of Proudhon's
ideas on the working class continued. He gave
to their subsequent endeavours another direction,
and separated the workmen's associations from
all communistic theories, and from all ideas of
revolutionary dictatorship.

CHAPTER IX.

PROUDHON was also the first who pointed out
that the only practical way to achieve the abolition of the political State-machinery would be by
the adoption of the Federative principle by the
Revolutionary party. He published, therefore,
an appeal to the Revolutionists urging them to
reorganise their party on a federal basis. His
ideas on the federal reorganisation of society
have now been adopted by the extreme fraction
in many countries; and, in fact, the present
struggle in Spain turns on the question whether
the Spanish Republic shall be another sterile
attempt to reconcile two irreconcilable principles—authority and liberty; or whether a new
system shall be inaugurated which shall neither
subordinate authority to liberty, nor liberty to
authority—antagonisms which have long vexed
mankind—but shall establish society on an
entirely new basis—a political contract. The
Calvinists invented the fiction of a social contract, subsequently adopted by J. J. Rousseau
and the Jacobins, in order to place the authority

of the Government on another foundation than
divine right.

The Federal principle, as imagined by Proudhon, and afterwards introduced into their systems
by French, Spanish, and Swiss Radicals, does
not rest on the fiction of a social contract, but is
a positive fact capable of modification at the
hands of the contracting parties. There is nothing in common between the Federal principle
as understood by Proudhon and his followers,
and the scheme of a European confederation
under the name of the United States of Europe,
which would comprise the existing European
states under the permanent presidency of a
congress. This was the scheme of the modern
Jacobins; but it was open to the objections, that
by giving to each state a number of votes in
proportion to its population, the dangers arising
from the conformation of the present political
system were maintained, and the sovereignty of
the individual is destroyed by establishing in
each state a government moulded in conformity
with past experience.

Nor was the constitution of the United States
of America considered to arrive at the ideal of a
realisation of the Federal principle. Turgot,
Mirabeau, Mably, Price, and others, had already
pointed out at the commencement of the American
Republic how strongly developed was the spirit

of aristocracy, regulating caste and privilege in
its organisation ; and hence it was natural that
such a constitution should be rejected by the
Federalist party founded by Proudhon.

The Swiss Constitution of the 12th September
1848, as subsequently amended, was the only
one Proudhon regarded as even an approach to
the realisation of the Federal principle. To him
the ideal state of society is that one in which
the political functions are reduced to mere commercial fractions, and where social order results
simply from transactions and exchange.

Every one would then be the autocratic ruler
of himself, and this constitutes the extreme antithesis to monarchical government. Proudhon
goes back to the first historical manifestations
of society in order to explain his ideas on self-
government pushed to the extreme. He recalled
the ancient " Mai-felder " of the Germans, in
which the whole people, without distinction of
age or sex, deliberated and gave their opinions ;
he spoke of the welfare of the Cimbrians and
Teutons, who, accompanied by their wives,
fought against Marius, uncommanded by any
general. In the judgments passed upon criminals in ancient Athens by the whole mass of the
citizens, he discovered the same antipathy of
popular instinct to all government; and he even
beheld a similar aspiration in the Republic of

1848, which appointed 900 legislators, as it was impossible to unite in one assembly the ten millions of French electors.

The Federal principle is to Proudhon and his modern followers the only means whereby existing states may be changed into an organisation which would almost amount to an abolition of the State. The following is the view held by him on this subject: The central Federal authority has but a limited range of action affecting only general measures; but its attributes cannot extend beyond those of the communal and provisional authorities which they centralise, and the latter cannot exceed the limits established by the rights of the individual citizens.

The Federal principle is therefore the exact reverse of the administrative centralisation of states on the unitarian principle.

In a federal republic the citizens create the State by a real contract (and not by the fiction of a social contract), the essential condition of which is that the members of the State retain a greater portion of their sovereignty in proportion as they abandon to the State. In any other form of State-organisation, monarchical or republican, which is not based upon Federation, the citizens give up their sovereign rights into the hands of an imperial or chosen authority. In a federal republic the central authority is also entrusted

with the public administration of the affairs of
the State, but only so far as it concerns Federal
services. But even this function is subordinate
to the constant control of the States of the
Federation, which can not only veto any of its
acts, but also possesses full and unrestrained
executive and judicial sovereignty in all matters
concerning its own existence. The Federal
principle alone can entirely abolish all dema-
gogic agitation, although the contrary is generally held. If, for instance, a revolution breaks
out in Paris, it could in no way react upon Lyons
or any other town of France. Gustave Chaudey,
one of the victims of the Paris commune, thus
described the Federal principle years before the
commune came into existence : " The ideal of
a confederation will be a treaty of alliance, of
which it can be said that it only imposes upon
the special sovereignties of the Federal States
such restrictions as become, in the hands of the
Federal authority, an extension of the guarantees
for the liberty of the citizens, and an increase of
protection for their individual or collective activity. By that alone the immense difference
existing can be understood between a federal
authority and a unitarian government, which
latter represents a single sovereignty."

Chaudey explains that in a federation centralisation is limited to certain general objects,

apart from the central sovereignty; it is therefore partial, whilst in a unitarian government
centralisation extends to everything, and is
therefore universal. Thus in Switzerland there
is a federal budget which relates solely to the
general affairs of the Confederation, but has no
connection with the budgets of the cantons or
communes.

The Federal Council could only exclude the
Jesuits from the whole of Switzerland, because a
special article of the Constitution authorised such
a measure. Otherwise every separate canton could
exercise its sovereignty so far as to retain the
Jesuits in its territory. Every canton of Switzerland can legislate on any possible subject which
is not specially reserved by the articles of the
Constitution for federal legislation. In some
countries the utility or otherwise of Monasteries
and Convents to the State has been discussed
by the national representatives. In Switzerland
their maintenance or abolition is reserved for cantonal legislation. Public opinion in Switzerland
is hostile to gambling-houses, but the National
Assembly could not compel the canton of Vaud
to share their views; consequently the town of
Saxon-les-Bains, in this canton, is the only one in
which these establishments are openly permitted
to exist. We may imagine an English county
possessing a certain autonomy, but Parliament

could at any moment enact a law abolishing this self-government. In Switzerland this could only be effected by an amendment of the Constitution, sanctioned not only by its representatives, but also ratified by the whole people. The sovereignty of the individual is more valued in Switzerland than a reform, which, though emphatically good in itself, could only be effected by a sacrifice of uniformity, and by the creation of a National Assembly, as a sovereign power.

Another instance. A special article of the Federal Constitution was required before the Federal Government could authorise the establishment of a federal university. Had that not been passed, the creation of the University of Zurich would have been impossible by the Swiss Parliament.

It would be impossible for Federal legislation to enact that instruction should be compulsory and gratuitous in every canton, or to impose secular education without receiving power to do so by a special amendment of the Constitution; but in a state based upon unitarian centralisation, the central legislative and executive authorities can make any changes that may seem good to them, and individual and collective rights are therefore never safe. The Swiss Federal Constitution of 1848 grants to every canton the right to modify its own constitution, provided that such a modification is of a progressive nature. Therefore the central power in Switzerland is not armed with a sovereign authority which may be exercised against the will of any one portion of the Confederation ; but, on the contrary, it has only been invested with a sovereign power in order that that power may be invoked by the minority of any single canton to protest against any infringement of their rights by the cantonal government.

The central power in Switzerland has been very accurately compared to the insurance of a house against fire. The authors of the most revolutionary constitution France ever possessed —viz., the one of 1793—went so far as to place it under the patriotism of the citizens, and in support of this measure even proclaimed the right of insurrection. Such a guarantee, however, was but a mere illusion ; whilst in Switzerland the State is composed of independent provinces, each guaranteeing the liberties of the other. France, whose mission it was in 1793 politically to reorganise mankind, did not consider the German confederation of single sovereign despots, or the Swiss Confederation, at that time purely aristocratic, nor even the American Confederation, in which the English model was too much maintained, as offering any inducements to the adoption of the Federal principle ; and the

Abbé Sieyes was the father of the unitarian system of liberal constitutions on the Continent.

Every trace of provincial independence was
abolished, and a new geographical division of
France was invented to crush the existing federalist ideas, which were regarded as harbouring
a counter-revolution. The Girondists, who
represented Federalism, were, in fact, far more
revolutionary than the Jacobins, who were
fanatics of centralisation. France, which had
declared herself a republic " une et indivisible,"
could not allow the neighbouring Swiss Republic
to exist on federal principles, and the Federal
Republic in Switzerland was therefore transformed into a unitarian republic. Since 1848,
Switzerland presents, however, in many respects,
the ideal realisation of the federal principle.

But even the Federal Constitution of 1815 was a
near approach to democratic federalism, and the
very name "Bundes*vertrag*" shows that the principle of " contract " was laid down as the basis
of the political organisation. The appellation
of the members of the Diet, "Bundes*gesandte*"
(ambassadors), implied the sovereign power of the
cantons, from whom they received an imperative
mandate on their appointment to the Diet.

In another point also did the Swiss Constitution realise the federal principle. There was
neither a president nor a federal council; but the

cantonal governments of those cantons in which
the Diet alternately met was during the session
entrusted with the presidency, and their officers
were entrusted with the execution of the resolutions passed by the Diet. Still more purely
does the Swiss Constitution represent this since
1848, inasmuch as it represents the idea of an
abolition of political State-machinery.

Centuries before Jesus Christ, the Jewish
tribes, separated by their valleys, were united by
a pact or federal contract, which alone can be
considered as an expression of political freedom.
In ancient Greece, too, the same federalist idea
prevailed; and the Teutonic, Sclavonian, and
Italian small states were likewise held together
by a federal principle.

But as federalism means liberty, and as discipline was in former times required to be brought
to bear upon the mass of the people, it was reserved to modern Switzerland to reconcile for
the first time liberty and authority.

In the United States of America the tendency has constantly been to increase the attributes of the federal authority, because the aim
of the Government has been more and more
directed towards political unity and centralisation. The President of the Federal Council of
Switzerland has neither the power of sanction
nor of a prohibitive veto held by the President of

the United States : he has merely to execute the
resolutions of the national representation. He
has no ministers, as the Federal Council per-
forms all the administrative functions of the
State. He is simply elected every year by the
Assembly from among the members of the Federal Council to preside at the sittings of the
latter. He cannot, therefore, like the President
of the United States, consider himself as a rival
expression to Congress of the will of the people.

The executive power also being limited to carrying out the decisions of the National Assembly, ministerial crises and ministerial changes
are alike impossible ; and the judges, as well as
the members of the Federal Council, hold office
only for the same term as the National Assembly
endures—namely, three years. The President
has no personal initiative, as all proposals of the
Government are made in the name of the Federal
Council. The National Assembly is the highest
court of appeal, not only in legal matters, but
even against decisions or orders of the Federal
Government, which can by it be reversed.

In Switzerland, therefore, the State, as represented by the Government authorities, is simply
a public servant, and is deprived of all sovereign
power. There is no division of the legislative
and executive powers in a federal republic,
because there are no powers to divide. Far

K

more power is possessed by the citizens than by
the State, because the latter is represented rather
by cantons and communes than by any central
authority. The Federal budget does not amount
to one-third of the expenses required to carry
on the political life of the nation ; and more than
two-thirds of the taxes are not voted or disposed
of by the central authorities, but by the cantons
and communes.

The Swiss nation has thus entirely liberated
itself from the State, not only because there is
not the faintest monarchical remembrance, or the
smallest attribute of a sovereign to be found in
the President of its Government, but also because
its Parliamentary Assembly is not invested with
that affectation of omnipotency which is peculiar
to every other national representation.

Blackstone said of the English Parliament
that it could do everything except change a
woman into a man. A Swiss Parliament can
never do as it likes.   The smallest canton has the
same rights of autonomy as the largest : the
canton of Zurich, on the basis of its population,
sends thirteen representatives into the National
Council, the canton of Zug but one ; nevertheless, in the Council of States, both cantons are
represented by an equal number of representatives. The National Council, the Council of
States, and the Federal Council can only discuss

such general questions as are allotted to them by
the Constitution. An amendment to the Constitution requires ere it becomes valid to be accepted
not only by them, but also subsequently by a
majority of the Swiss nation. Neither the National Council nor the Cantonal Council can
interfere in communal affairs, since each commune in Switzerland possesses an autonomy
similar to that enjoyed in ancient times by
Athens, Rome, or Venice.

The principle of a federal republic has been
interpreted by Castelar and his Spanish friends
on a far wider scale than as it exists in Switzerland. The revision of the Constitution, which
was proposed to and rejected by the Swiss nation
last year, would, had it been passed, entirely
have broken the unitarian government, and for
ever have uprooted the danger of any personal
will influencing the destinies of the country.
Federal centralisation, or the State, would have
become a mere contract for a mutual guarantee ;
and each group, canton, or commune, would
have thus formed a state ruling and managing
its own affairs by universal suffrage.

Had the proposed revision of the Constitution
been carried, there would have been granted to
the whole of Switzerland what is now in existence in some of the cantons—viz., 1. The initiative of the people in legislation, according to

which any measure supported by 50,000 electors must *ipso facto* be taken into consideration by the National Council and the Council of State. 2. The *ad referendum* and *veto—i.e.*, that not only constitutional amendments, but also all other laws, should be submitted for sanction to the electors, who should have the right to reject them.

The proposed Federal Constitution was rejected by the electors; but it is certain to be brought forward again, not only in Switzerland, but also in Spain, where the idea of a Federal contract replacing the State has made great progress.

CHAPTER X.

LA REPUBLIQUE UNE ET INDIVISIBLE.

THE federative principle has not been generally adopted by French Democrats, who, for the most part, were in favour of the unitarian system. This fact, specially prominent at the time of the Italian war, was again, during the Paris Commune, remarkable, when the Jacobin traditions of a united and strong central government once more proved predominant in France.

When in 1789 monarchical absolutism was broken, France began at first to take up the federal principle. The battalions which were sent from all the provinces to Paris were called *federés;* and the *cahiers*, or voting instructions given to the deputies by the electors, were issued in the name of the " Etats," each province thus regarding itself as a state. Since then, however, the idea of a republic " une et indivisible " has become everywhere prevalent, and the war of Italy with France renewed the discussion of federal ideas with the French democracy. Ferrari declared in the Parliament of Turin, " If

the whole of Italy were to meet and tell me that
it was unitarian, I should still reply, ' You are
mistaken.' "   In France all democrats were in
favour of Italian unity : Proudhon was the only
representative of democracy who opposed the
unity of Italy with a fanaticism which went so
far that he even defended the temporal rule of
the Pope.   Nor was that all : he had the cour-
age to side with the Emperor, who wanted to
free Italy and afterwards to confederate it ; he
attacked Garibaldi and Mazzini, and quarrelled
with the whole liberal press of France and Bel-
gium, which had pronounced in favour of Italian
unity.

Garnier-Pagès and Desmarets were the only
politicians in France who defended the principle
of a European confederation, though they did
not go so far as Proudhon, whose opinions were
but timidly reproduced by Villiaume, who, in a
pamphlet entitled " Le Salut de l'Italie," explained also, from a democratic stand-point, that
the mission of Italy was to inaugurate liberal
progress by confederation.

The Paris Commune was a second opportunity
for testing the advocates of the federal principle.
The idea of the Paris Commune was stained by
the wild and lawless deeds of its members ; but
at the root of it lay that germ of an organisation
of society which deprives the national represen-

tation of its sovereign power, and brings it into
healthy, vigorous connection with the communal and departmental representation, even as
a stone cast into a clear sheet of water produces
similar but ever-widening circles. This conception of the commune as the egg of society, whose
office it was to assimilate communal and state
affairs, and thus to import the whole nation
into the Government, was not understood. History proves that society can be organised on
such a basis without losing its unity. A profound student of ancient Roman society called it
a federation of families, and even the Middle
Ages have been regarded by the more careful
historians as representing society based on contracts for mutual services. Guizot says, "There
were not in the associations of the possessors of
fiefs either subjects or citizens." Dupont-White
has indeed divided the contracts created by
feudal society into three classes — the feudal
engagement, the contract between the serfs
themselves, and the letter of exchange inaugurated by the Jews. Both financially and politically, feudal society was therefore based on a
distinct and actual contract, and not on a fiction.
Even amid all the abuses of the old French
monarchy, there was yet one peculiarity which
might be interpreted as vaguely establishing the
identity of the State and the individual. For

centuries England struggled to limit the power
of the Government, whilst in France the tendency to participate in the Government was more
distinguishable.

This is the real explanation of the place-
hunting which has always characterised the
French nation, since everybody desires to become part and parcel of the Government. For
the same reason it was possible that in France,
even up to a recent period, Government offices
could be bought and sold.   Franklin interpreted
this fact from a higher point of view, and in his
letters he says : " Justice is administered very
cheaply in France, and even for nothing ; since
the members of the Parliament buy their offices,
and do not make more than three per cent. of
their money by their salary and other emolu-
ments, while legal interest is five per cent.   It
may be said that they give all their time and
their trouble for two per cent. to be allowed to
govern."

And the prices given for these offices were
enormous.   In 1639, sixteen *maîtres des re-
quêtes* were appointed, and the right of filling
these offices was sold for sixteen millions of
francs.   Towns would purchase the rights of
incorporation and to form guilds, and the Tiers-
Etat grew principally by the purchase of offices.
Nothing was more obstinately defended than the

right of the individual to purchase the right of
ruling his fellow. Even against Richelieu was
the right maintained, since, before raising the
citadel of the Ile de Rhe, he was compelled to
pay 100,000 crowns to the Comte de Toiras, who
had bought the governorship of the island.

Dupont-White has pointed out that the French
Revolution displayed at first a similar tendency
to liberty by granting the greatest possible
amount of participation in the Government. The
first article of the Constitution of 1791 is as
follows :—

" All citizens are admissible to places and
employments without any other distinction but
that of virtue."

Subsequent French constitutions repeated this
article.

Revolutionary movements in other countries
had given rise to cries for the partition of land,
for tribunes, for an annual votation of taxes, for
a Habeas Corpus Act, &c. ; but in France the
national weakness for office-seeking was based
on a general misunderstanding of the State.

Throughout our entire work we have principally had in view the French people, because,
politically, France has always been the nation
which has experimentalized for the general
benefit of mankind. A continuous convulsion of
ideas—extreme, unhealthy, almost caricaturist

views concerning the relations of the State and
the individual—permeate the whole history of
France. The controversy between the upholders
of the *état-maitre* and the *état-serviteur* existed
even in former centuries in France. Montesquieu, who so thoroughly understood the
social science that it was rightly said of him
that he rediscovered the title-deeds of the human
race, was the originator of the doctrine, " the
right of work," which in our days has been
chiefly defended by Louis-Blanc.

He says in his " Esprit des Lois : "—

" In commercial countries, where most of the
people have nothing but their trades, the State
is often obliged to provide for the wants of old
men, invalids, and orphans. A well-organised
State draws the means for achieving this from the
trades themselves; it gives to these the work they
are capable of performing, and to those it gives
instructions how to work, which of itself is work.
Alms given to a naked man in the streets do
not fulfil the obligation of the State, which ought
to provide every citizen an assured subsistence,
proper food, and clothes, and a way of getting
his living not contrary to the requirements of
health."

This school would have all progress emanate from the State, and points out how the
nomad Tartars and Arabs, who have, down to the

present day, maintained this original form of
society for more than three thousand years, are,
with their groups of families and tribes, no further in the path of advancement than they were
in the most ancient times; whilst the State,
even when it neglects progress for itself, still
initiates it by every action. What does it matter that Louis XI., in establishing posts, only
had in view the transport of his own letters? or
that another government expatriates its felons,
and thus establishes a colony? or that in some
portions of France the roads were merely con-
structed for military purposes, when they at the
same time served for the conveyance of mer-
chandise and produce?

The Royal Printing-Office in Paris was originally opened only for printing the " Bulletin des
Lois;" but in this instance, as in many others,
the State, according to this school, always sets an
example, even when it does not render a service.

When Napoleon I. instituted the Bank of
France, his intention was, according to Dupont-
White, to bring the capitalists under his thumb,
and place them at his disposal; but, at the same
time, not less did he give an immense impulse to
commerce and production.

This school has a positive fanaticism for the
State; they yearn for authority, and they re-
mind us of Henri IV. of France, who on his

return to Paris said, " Let the people approach
me—they are starving for the sight of a king!"
Some of its members ought almost to live on the
Viti Islands, where, according to missionaries,
the natives are divided into two castes, the eat-
able and the eating castes.   The most important
modern philosophers of the State-worship are
De Bonald, who used the words " dependance
et paternité" as a motto of the State, instead
of " liberté, egalité, et fraternité;" and De
Maistre, who held that "the people is always
foolish, distracted, and childish, and requires a
guardian."

It is but natural that beside such fanatics,
whose every pore seemed permeated with a love of
governing, there were other fanatics who regarded
society as a mere collection of individuals; and
it is a remarkable fact that Frederick Bastiat,
who was so greatly opposed to Proudhon in
his views on national economy, agreed with
him entirely in hatred of laws.   The severest
reproach Bossuet addressed to Luther was not
based on religious grounds, but on the reformer's
words, that man must not be the subject of man;
and what is more especially strange is the fact
that this political doctrine of Luther found more
favour in Catholic than in Protestant countries;
and the anti-state movements of the early Protestant leaders are frequently quoted by the

modern French school of abolitionists of the State authority.

The first protest against State and laws did not in France emanate from the Revolutionary party. There is not a wild attack against laws, not an attempt to uproot old customs, kings, institutions, ay, even to abolish the right of property itself, but can be found in the pages of Pascal. He despises abuses quite as much as reforms; he tramples under foot the whole State; he even despises human reason, to find, after all, a refuge in religion.

Bastiat in our own times also played thus with fire. He it was, a conservative thinker, who defined society as a collection of individuals, and who subsequently destroyed the authority of the State in these words, which he added to his definition: "There exist no more rights in this collection than there are in its component parts. Individuals can only use force in legitimate defence. Therefore the collection of individuals, the State (which is the same thing), only has the right to put down violence and fraud; such repression being the sole use of force which can be regarded as legitimate defence."

Even Guizot, in his "History of Civilisation," acknowledged that real progress goes on apart from the State. He said: "C'est aujourd'hui une remarque vulgaire, qu'à mesure que la

civilisation et la raison font des progrès, cette
classe de faits sociaux qui sont étrangers à toute
necessité extérieure à l'action de tout pouvoir
public, devient de jour en jour plus large et plus
riche. La société non gouvernée, la société qui
subsiste par le libre developement de l'intelli-
gence et de la volonté humaine, va toujours s'éten-
dant à mesure que l'homme se perfectionne.
Elle devient de plus en plus le fonds social."

Guizot conceived, therefore, the existence of a
species of freemasonry of chosen men, for whom
the State could not exist, because they were
civilised enough to escape it, but who could not
admit that ever a time would come when society
in general would repose on the Federal principle
and do without any sovereign authority:

Thus much has the protest against all political authority been developed in France and
Spain since the time of Guizot. It is sufficient
for a government to be established in Paris, and
an opposition party is at once created. On the
24th February 1848, the party of the " National " was considered as the extreme political
party in France; on the following day a party
existed by whom the " Nationalists " were looked
upon as reactionary, because they were satisfied
with the Republican form of government, and
the new opposition declared that Socialism must
henceforth be the object of society.

It is related of Proudhon that he desired a world where he would be guillotined as a reactionist. Although said but jestingly, yet this statement exactly illustrates the increase of the anti-governmental idea in France. A member of the Paris Commune went so far as to propose that France should be divided into a number of small states, or rather communes, each independent of the other, and only united by a treaty of alliance offensive and defensive, with the obligation in addition of supplying a certain contingent of soldiers for the general defence. In this scheme for the abolition of Government, the army is retained as the only natural bond of union.

Spanish Federal Republicans, on the other hand, desired to break down the military frame of iron in which the State was set; and General Pierrard, who was attached to the Ministry of War which came into office immediately after the abdication of King Amadeus, addressed an official circular to the " autonomic and decentralised army," for which he received an ovation from the Intransigents, who sent a deputation to congratulate him on his ideas.

The incident of the Samana Bay Company, which reduced the idea of a sovereign government still more to the level of a joint-stock company, even as was the case with the East

India Company, contributed not a little to deprive the idea of government of its original character. So many governments had been upset, so many dynasties driven away, that the pure conception of a government was spoiled.

It is easy to understand that the present political organisation of the State appears to many no longer absolutely necessary, as the municipal idea becomes more and more developed and appreciated. We can, for instance, imagine London existing for itself, and without any ministry or parliament in its midst, and with only a mayor, common council, police, and the other existing local institutions. Excellent order would doubtless be maintained in the metropolis, and it would equally continue to hold its present position in the national life.

If Liverpool, Manchester, Birmingham, and all the other towns and villages, were, one after the other, raised up into the air, and utterly disunited from the State of England, it can easily be imagined that each separate city, town, or village would lead a non-political life; and those persons who advocate the suppression of all State-machinery declare, that in order to understand the idea of a state without government, one has only to imagine each separated particle again put together, and made once more to form a homogeneous whole. The entirety would then exist as before, though utterly deprived of all political government.

How many millions are there in every country who hardly know of the existence of their Parliaments, or at all events are utterly ignorant of what goes on in them, or what their representatives are doing on their behalf! They live only to be governed, and the State circle does not therefore comprise all the inhabitants, but only a few members of political factions. Oxenstierna let out the secret of the government trick when he said on his deathbed, " My son, how little wisdom is required to govern the world ! "

Nothing is more difficult in actual practice than to lop off the smallest limb from that huge Moloch—the State. It takes centuries to modify any form of State, and it is therefore hardly necessary to add that all these speculations for the entire suppression of the State-frame are but theories. But these theories, although of no immediate practical value, are not to be despised ; and much can be learned from them which might increase our self-reliance, our individual dignity, and our comprehension of liberty, and at the same time diminish our inveterate craving for authority and our worship of idols.

L

CHAPTER XI.

CONCLUSION.

WE must now conclude. We have been here chiefly engaged in describing the hotbed of democracy in France, but at some future opportunity we may be able to give an account of analagous movements in other countries, with especial reference to the leaders of the Spanish Federalist Republicans. We also hope to be enabled to explain in a special work the financial radicalism of continental democracy, and we shall then more fully describe Proudhon's scheme of a " Banque du Peuple."

To some the ideas expressed in the foregoing pages may appear Utopian and even anarchical, but at the root of all these lies a great thought of human liberty.

Nothing is so difficult to understand as liberty, because for centuries mankind has regarded State and society, religion and the Church, as identical. Only those persons are really free—and there have been such men in all ages—who lived outside the trammels of the State, and only regarded themselves as a link in the endless chain of the universe. The monstrosity of this view, even on abstract philosophical grounds, appears astounding and perplexing. The greatest minds have felt themselves solitary and helpless in this mysterious night illumined only by countless stars, and have, like Kant, announced the necessity of a philosophical orthodoxy which they called postulates of practical reason.

The free man could in this spiritual region be contented with the abstract idea of God, he could in fact deny the Godhead and find a solution of the problem in the absolute idea, which is represented and embodied in the universe. The unfree man shudders at this formless black mysterious medium, he needs a crutch to preserve him from falling into the abyss of thought, and thus it was easy for the prophets to found a religion. Even the most uncouth idol was eagerly worshipped by unfree millions, as a salvation from the awful, dreadful mystery of the universe. Prayer responded intellectually to their slavish needs, and it is only a really strong man who can imagine a society without a Church and even aim at such a condition of affairs.

As the Church has become the guardian and the director of the philosophical gifts of mankind, even so has society transformed itself into the State with its inexorable forms because it abhorred freedom. The royal idea is in the social what

the divine idea is in the philosophical sphere.
To the unfree individual, political government is
as necessary as the Church. Those men who
do not comprehend liberty and the individual,
singularly enough, are far easier reconciled to
religious than political atheism. They hold it a
lesser danger to live with people who deny God
than with those who deny the State. To them it
seems as easy to live without some form of state
as to jump out of their skins. The philosophically
unfree man regards the resistance to priestcraft
as the highest development of religious enlighten-
ment, and believes that in a republic the greatest
political liberty is to be found: as if a republican
government was a' whit more associated with
true liberty than any other political government.

It is so difficult to understand liberty that we
run the risk of preaching anarchy and barbarism,
if only we discuss the possibility of abolishing
the State. Sham liberalism has its " non
possumus " just as has the Papacy, and in its
eyes those persons are regarded as deprived of
reason who declare every parliamentary representation of the people, and every government,
as phases of the social organisation, which at
some time or another must be overcome. A
radical republican or a revolutionary dictator
would hold him foolish who should attempt to
point out that he as little understood or realised

liberty as the most absolute sultan or autocrat. Modern democracy would consider it downright heresy to regard manhood suffrage and secret voting as only a new form of serfdom, because they are only means to re-establish a government and a political representation.

It has been the object of these pages to introduce to our readers in short general terms those men who have held that Parliamentarism is merely an abdication of the sovereignty of the people and of liberty, and that free men can neither be represented nor governed. Abolition of the State means only the suppression of all *political* government, and every *political* popular representation, and the abrogation of the *political* constitution.

Is it possible to replace the State by free society without deteriorating into barbarism? Was the original patriarchal social tie which even now obtains amongst certain wild races, barbaric? or does barbarism disappear with the commencement of the State? This is the problem which a succession of men, who do not shrink from liberty, and who believe that social conservation would be more easily and safely achieved by simple centralisation, and management by delegates of material interests, than by any political power, have for centuries sought to solve.

The defenders of the Federal Republic in
Spain are already approaching the idea of replacing the State by an unpolitical parochial
administration ; the efforts of Switzerland to
make all legislation dependent on the ratification
of the people are also a step in the direction of
the view that the people cannot be represented,
and that a parliamentary constitution is incompatible with true liberty. The men who considered the total suppression of the State machine
to be possible, have been hitherto regarded as were
those persons who, at the beginning of the present
century, talked of railways, locomotives, and
telegraphs. Railways and locomotives had long
existed ere the idea arose of .combining the two.
Just as at the present time there are many
people who are willing to substitute a general
armament of the people for the army, but who
yet would declare it to be perfectly impossible
to do away with the ministry of war. If social
interests make it necessary to establish an armament of the people, the institution of volunteers
or even of a self-imposed compulsory service can
obviously replace the political tool called an
army. If in addition thereto it were also possible to replace the political office of war minister
by a simple delegate, who should merely be
elected by the body corporate of the people, in
order to look after the military interests of free

society, one portion of the Government would thus be suppressed without in any way affecting general social interests.

Chambers of Commerce even at the present time are only a social, non-political, unofficial arrangement which have been instituted by the requirements of trade interests. If it were possible to universalise these Chambers of Commerce and to centralise them, and to have a delegate elected by them, who, in accordance with a specified mandate, should watch over commercial interests generally, a second tooth would thus be extracted from the head of the State. The ministry of commerce would thus cease to exist, without the flood of barbarism overwhelming society. Already society is acquainted with parochial rates which are merely paid to furnish funds for the practical requirements of a parish, without any political *arrière-pensée*. Is it possible to place this taxation under the direct control of all the parishioners, and to make every parish contribute to the general expenditure which not only concerns them but the whole body of society? the delegate would, in that case, easily replace the ministry of finance, he having received the non-political mission to concentrate this general social expenditure, not under the indifferent control of a Parliamentary assembly, but under the control of communes directly interested, and therefore more likely thoroughly to watch over the general expenditure.

The material international relations of a free society, make consuls now necessary, officers of the State, who have to look after the interests of their own country in foreign lands, apart, however, from any political or diplomatic character. If, however, it were possible to go one step further, and to place the consuls under the central direction of an international administration, the political office of a minister of foreign affairs would thus be suppressed, and the abolition of the State would then be still further prepared.

· The example of the dissenters clearly proves that the State is in no way wanted to guard the religious interests of society.

The election of the judges by the people in America proves also that the abolition of the ministry of justice is possible ; in one word, free men aim at the suppression of the political council of ministers and its transformation into a centralising council of administration elected by the people. As republics exist the abolition of kingdoms must make a further step towards the abolition of the State possible. The question is then only, whether the political legislative assemblies, who regard themselves as representatives of popular sovereignty, can be suppressed.

The first clear abnegation of every political
representation emanated from J. J. Rousseau,
who says in his " Contrat Social : " " The sovereignty being. only the exercise of the general
will can never be alienated, and the sovereign
who is only a collective being, can only be represented by himself. The idea of representatives
is modern, and has descended to us from feudal
government, the ancient republics knew nothing
of it. The diminution of patriotism, the increased activity of private interest, the immensity
of States, conquests and abuses of governments,
have led to it. Nevertheless, the deputies
neither are or can be the representatives of the
people, they are only its commissioners, they
can conclude nothing definitively ; every law not
ratified by the people personally is void—it is
not a law. Directly a people gives itself representatives it is no longer free, it exists no
more."

The opposition to parliamentary assemblies
which pass laws and are supposed to represent
the sovereignty of the people, has since that
time increased extraordinarily, and this extreme
idea has chiefly been nourished in Switzerland
by the institution of the practice of *ad referendum.* But nowhere is parliamentarism so much
despised as in France. The representative
system itself sank into disrepute in consequence

of the corrupt Chamber of Deputies of Louis
Philippe, and since then its application to truly
democratic principles has generally been regarded
as an impossibility.

It was in fact declared impossible to delegate
the sovereignty, because the idea of the first is
absolute and of the second relative. The opposition was chiefly directed against a delegation of
the legislative power, because even the most
enlightened representatives were constantly
swayed in their public duties by private interest,
and it could not be said that the people gave
itself laws, when they were voted by its representatives. General as was the opposition to
legislative assemblies in the circles of extreme
democrats, equally general was the idea that
it was possible, and even necessary, to delegate
the executive or rather the administrative functions.

The staunchest defenders of national autonomy
admit that laws passed directly by the people
could only come into operation in the daily
details of civic life by means of one or several
individuals, but they desire that their action
should be non-political. They think it possible
to change the State into a species of joint-stock
company, the managers of which should have
extensive powers in the administration of the
material interests of the social shareholders, the

latter, however, remaining in every other respect their own masters.

For some time past, from every side, opposing elements have been pressing onward against the State. Not only is it the philosophical hermit, who, feeling his loneliness in every society,—ay, even in the universe itself,—clenches his fist against the State, but the workman and the man of the people who for centuries have patiently remained in the background, now make their demands of society, and moodily brooding before the monster, seek how best it may be overthrown.

In the political world there are extremes like Louis Napoleon and Bismark, who have been as strongly opposed to the restraints imposed by Parliamentary institutions as the veriest member of the Internationale, whose programme is a protest against present political institutions. It is not without significance that Bismark selected as his secretary Herr Bucher, the talented author of a book on "Parliamentarism." In France, the entire Republican party has adopted the custom of only electing those candidates who consent to receive a "*mandat imperatif*," and as soon as a Parliament consists only of members who have accepted such a "*mandat*," it at once loses its sovereign character.

During the last elections in Spain the electors

in many districts went even much further than
the "*mandat imperatif*," since they only voted
for those candidates who previously consented to
sign a document containing their resignation,
the date of which was to be filled in by the
electors whenever they should feel themselves
dissatisfied with the parliamentary services of
their representative, whom they could thus at
any moment compel to relinquish his seat.
These deputies are called "*Pignadores.*"

The Republic had but few supporters in Spain
when the revolution which drove out Queen
Isabella II. broke out in 1868.   It was in
Catalonia that the Spanish Republican party
originated, and one of its chief apostles in 1842-3
was a man named Obolon Ferradas, who died in
exile.   Figueras Pi and the other Catalonian
Republicans were his disciples.   Orense, too,
was among the first believers in these advanced
doctrines, as also was the Marquis d'Albaida,
who may almost be termed the patriarch of the
Republican party in Spain.

The repressive measures of the Government,
which put down the freedom of the press and
the right of public meeting, prevented the pro-
pagation of Republican doctrines until the year
1868. . The faction existed under the name of
the Democratic party, and apparently aspired

more to the acquisition of individual rights than to change the form of government.

Some of the principal speakers and writers, among others Rivèro and Martos, who fought in the ranks of the Republicans, so soon as those rights were established, gave in their adhesion to the monarchical form of government and served King Amadeus.

Every one must be struck with the wonderful rapidity with which the Republican party has sprung up in Spain. How is it that that party has developed in a country which has been so essentially monarchical from the remotest ages? It is only by the force of circumstances that great ideas are born : no party in any country is originated in a day. Neither history or the natural course of events can show a similar instance to what occurred in Spain.

What took place there is a political phenomenon, of which the following is the explanation. The revolution of September was effected, as is well known, by a coalition of Liberal fractions, that is to say, by the Progressist party, under the leadership of Prim, and by the party of the Liberal Union, headed by Marshal Serrano.

When Orense, Castelar, Pi, and others, who were then known as democrats, returned to Spain after an enforced absence of two years, the revolution was complete. None of the chiefs of the

Republican party had had any hand in the plots which preceded that revolution,—plots which, thanks principally to the diplomacy of Olozaga, had been confined to the Unionists and Progressists; and some of the Republicans were even ignorant of what was going on, and the means employed were carefully concealed from them.

The Progressist and Unionist parties, personified by Prim and Serrano, agreed on one point, the most important of all: the dethronement of Isabella. Both were monarchists, and if they did not proclaim a monarchy in the first moments of their triumph, it was not because they were doubtful of the monarchical feeling of the majority of the country, or from a fear of a Republican party, which at that time had no existence, but simply because they could not agree as to who should be the occupant of the throne from which they had driven Isabella. That was the real reason which induced them to form a Provisional Government until the meeting of the Constituent Cortes. That sort of truce between two parties, each of which had a different candidate in view, was equally convenient to both.

The Liberal Unionist party, which was in favour of the Duke of Montpensier, determined to allow some time to elapse in order to allay the popular sentiment of hostility which pre-

vailed against all the members of the late reign-
ing family; while the Progressist party, the
leaders of which desired the realisation of an
Iberian Kingdom by the union of Spain with
Portugal, gladly welcomed a delay which thus
gave them time to prepare a scheme for the can-
didature of either the King of Portugal or his
father Dom Fernando.

The truth of the matter was, that on the 29th
of September 1868, the day of the triumph of
the revolution at Madrid, Spanish Republicans
were very scarce. Many a voice might on that
day have been heard shouting "Down with
Isabella," but never one cried "Long live the
Republic."

Certain it is that one of the chief causes of
the development of the Republican idea was this
delay, agreed upon by the Progressists and Unionists, and the formation of a Provisional Government, which allowed all kinds of unaccustomed
liberty, such as of the press and of public meeting, as well as all kinds of demonstrations—liberties, in fact, which gradually assumed a Republican character.

Hence it came to pass that the populations of
the large towns, which were not in favour of an
absolute monarchy, like the Carlists, because from
education they had a traditional hatred of Don
Carlos, and who could not continue to be constitu-

tionally monarchical because they had no king, even prospectively, began to believe in the possibility of a Republican form of Government in Spain.

The ground was thus prepared when the Republican speakers and newspapers began to disseminate their doctrines. The germination was prompt, almost instantaneous. Scarcely was the Revolution of 1868 triumphant in Spain when Orense and Pi-y-Margall, re-entering the country from exile, issued a manifesto in which they boldly unfurled the Federal Republican flag.

That also coincided with the return of Castelar, who, in the first Spanish town wherein he set his foot, viz., Irun, made a speech in favour of the Republic.

In the provinces the second-rate orators responded to the attitude assumed by the now returned Republicans, by convoking meetings and starting journals, at which and in which, the principles of Federalism were openly advanced.

Liberal people who found themselves in the position above indicated, and only waited for a banner, enthusiastically greeted that of the Republic; and hence it was that in a few days a party, already powerful, appeared in Andalusia, Catalonia, and in the old kingdom of Valencia.

But how came it to pass that the party favoured a Federal rather than a Unitarian republic?

The truth is, that before the Revolution not one
of the few Republicans then existing, with the
exception of one or two men who were pledged to
support the Federal form, had come to any
decided opinion upon the point.

Orense was one of these exceptions. In his
conversations with his friends, and even in some
of his writings, he had extolled the Federal idea,
basing its utility on the diversity of origin,
customs, and even languages, prevailing in the
various ancient divisions of Spanish territory,
and more particularly on the fact that a Federal
Republic was the one which offered the greatest
prospect of stability, in that it afforded no open-
ing for a dictatorship.

Castelar, who left Spain in 1866, and had long
resided at Geneva, had been vividly impressed
with the organisation of the Helvetian Republic,
and with such a pattern before him he evolved
in his mind an ideal Spanish Republic. Castelar, a man of lively and exceedingly impression-
able imagination, probably owes to his stay at
Geneva his strong views on the organisation of
the Republic.

As regards Pi-y-Margall, he is a warm disciple
and admirer of Proudhon, whose works he has
translated, and he is said to have acquired his
Federalist opinions during his sojourn in Paris.
The example of an empire emanating from a

Unitarian Republic clearly showed him the disadvantage of that form of government, and hence his, like Orense's, preference for Federalism, as offering greater stability and less danger.

For the mass of the Spanish people, they but follow the guidance of their leaders.

The real national chief of the Federal party in Spain is Señor Orense, and his followers have taken the name of Central Reformists. They are opposed to the more moderate section of the Federalists originally organised by Figueras, and known as the " New Centre." A compromise between these two centres appears, at the time we write, impossible, owing to the personal influence of Figueras being now at an end. The executive committee of the Central Reformists is composed of Orense, Somolinos, J. J. Mena, F. Sicilia, J. M. Cabello del la Vega, J. Navarridi, and A. L. Cairion. There is no doubt that the final object these Central Reformists have in view is the seizure of the lands now held by the great feudal landowners, and their redistribution among the people, by which means they hope to fan the flame of patriotism by giving to each peasant who may thus become an owner of land a stake in the country—a course successfully pursued by the French Convention in the days of the revolution of 1793. As also,

by assignats, the French Government of that
time sought to relieve the financial embarrass-
ment of the country, so also the Central Reformists of the present day hope, by the emission
of paper money, based on the proceeds of the
sale of government lands, to detach the country
from the banking monopolists of the commercial
world, and to rely entirely upon the financial
resources of the people, and finally, by repudiating the public debt acquired by the monarchy, they declare war to the financial world. So
far the Orensist party repeats the programme of
the Convention as regards the crown, church,
land, and finances. Several points of their
scheme are but simple amplifications of the
"*Droits de l'homme.*" We have only here to
introduce the main points of Orense's programme
to prove how entirely the Federalists intend to
break down feudalism, monarchism, and class
privileges. These are as follows :—

The rights inherent to human personality hold
the front rank in the Constitution, and are acknowledged to be anterior and superior to any
law.

These rights are exercised by all men on Spanish territory, whether natives or foreigners.

They can never be suspended or limited by
the public powers.

Capital punishment is abolished.

Criminals will undergo imprisonment on certain islands of the Spanish colonies.

Slavery is abolished in Spanish territory. The Cuban slaves will be free on the proclamation of the present law.

Suppression of all official salaries.

Equal civil rights for men and women.

Any abuse of power injurious to any human being will be indemnified by the national treasury without prejudice to the responsibility of the guilty party.

Justice will be administered gratuitously in Spanish territory.

The public powers are independent. The legislative power remains distinct from the executive and judicial powers.

Of the executive power the civil and military branches are distinct.

The position of deputies is incompatible with any salaried public position.

The secret police is suppressed.

Every proprietor must contribute to the public charges in proportion to the services which he receives from society.

A period of one month is allowed for all proprietors to declare the real value of their property. After that time any property not truly declared, or the difference stated between the real and declared value or extent of any property, will be considered national property.

The State holds no monopolies, but simply public services, which should not be a source of profit.

Periodicals and books sent by railway are free from stamp duty.

Fishing and shooting licences are abolished.

The Council of State, Council of Foreign Affairs, Superior Tribunals of War and Marine, the Admiralty, and the Supreme Tribunal of Police, are abolished.

Lotteries are abolished.

Captaincies-General are suppressed.

All arsenals and arm manufactories of the State will be sold. All the fortified places on the Portuguese frontier will be razed to the ground.

One great difference, however, exists between the Convention and the Central Reformists of Spain. The Convention aimed at the unity of the State—state dictatorship, government guardianship, government power and rule—whilst the Spanish Federalists are to supply the first precedent in history of a country relinquishing its unity after having for centuries worked to overcome provincialism. Orense's party is therefore the first practical expression of an endeavour to abolish the State; and as soon as the real intentions of the " Intransigentes " shall become known in Spain, the split in the aristo-

cracy, which occurred at the ascension of the
throne by Isabella II., will cease, and, in fact,
there will be but two parties in Spain—one the
State party, and the other the anti-State party,
the latter not only impugning the government
of man by man, but also the social and financial
" *exploitation de l'homme par l'homme.*"   France
has therefore fulfilled her mission as the battle-
field of modern democracy against feudalism,
and Switzerland and Spain will next try the
experiment of carrying on the struggle on a new
basis.

But many other signs are cropping up throughout Europe of national life being no longer
expressed by parliaments and governments.
The French National Assembly is in no degree
in accord with the great body of the people.
Here also, in England, the House of Lords has
long been little better than a constitutional fiction; and it remains to be seen if, in the next
general election, the House of Commons will
veritably and organically connect itself with the
working-classes, or whether it will socially be as
foreign to the hopes, fears, desires, and aspira-
tions of the masses as politically is the case
with the Versailles Assembly.

This scheme for the reorganisation of society
may be considered as a dream by many, but at
the root of it there lies a proud intuition of the

rights of the individual and a protest against all guardianship and unnecessary authority. It opens before us a view of a free unfettered human civilisation, and we obtain from it a glimpse of an entirely new organisation of society, which deserves a serious examination even at the hands of adversaries. Frequently those persons who appear to be preachers of anarchy and disorder, are in reality aiming at a higher condition of social order than the one at present existing. When first constitutional representative government was demanded, it seemed monstrous to those who held from habit that mankind could only exist beneath a despotism. Such a lesson of history ought to be well considered before an absolute anathema is pronounced on those who wrote in favour of an Abolition of the State.

THE END.

www.ingramcontent.com/pod-product-compliance
Lightning Source LLC
Chambersburg PA
CBHW030608040726
47497CB00008B/2893